T3-AOR-441

THE SEARCH
FOR TRUTH

THE SEARCH FOR TRUTH

•

Judy and Ronald Culp

AVALON BOOKS
NEW YORK

PRINTED IN THE UNITED STATES OF AMERICA
ON ACID-FREE PAPER
BY HADDON CRAFTSMEN, BLOOMSBURG, PENNSYLVANIA

To family and friends who
encourage and support us.

The journey is the thing.

Prologue

Lying on his belly in the loose gravel beside a granite boulder, the stranger's back was warmed by the late morning sunlight. Spreading his feet comfortably, he looked down the long barrel of his buffalo rifle at the tall young man standing on the stage-line office porch across the river. Drinking coffee, deep in conversation with an older man who wore a cook's apron, the young man threw back his head and laughed at something the other fellow was saying.

With practiced ease the stranger brought the tip of the front sight blade center and level in the "V" of the rear sight ladder he'd flipped up and set for three hundred and fifty yards. He took a deep breath, aware of the smell of the light oil he rubbed into the gunmetal every day, and let some air out as his finger took up the trigger slack. With the sights aligned low and centered on the young man's belt buckle, he squeezed the trigger smoothly. At the shot, the gun stock slammed hard into his shoulder, white smoke billowed, thinned, and drifted slowly away as the sound of his shot echoed across the valley, fading with distance like a dance in slow motion. Through the veil of smoke he saw the young man collapsing in a heap on the floor. The older man quick-

1

ly bent and dragged the dead body, for surely that's what it was, back into the building.

The stranger smiled in grim satisfaction at a deed well done. An easy hundred dollars, he thought as he ejected the spent brass cartridge case. Taking up his unfinished cigarette, he took one last puff. Grinding the smoldering butt into the dusty gravel, he walked to his horse, carefully put his rifle in the saddle scabbard, mounted, and rode up into the high country as silently as he had come.

Chapter One

Catherine Stone placed the last load of freshly laundered sheets on the rocky ground under the clothesline. The wash she'd done and hung out earlier had almost completely dried in the warm air pushed by fresh breezes down the high mountain valley. As she spread the first sheet across the line and pulled several clothespins from her apron pocket, she idly watched a rider galloping up the road that passed by her boarding house to climb the mountains toward Cottonwood Pass. The rider slowed to turn into the drive leading to her house, and, shading her eyes against the bright morning sun with a flattened hand, Catherine recognized him as Pastor Paul Fry, the circuit-riding preacher who served the towns in the valley. He usually stayed at Catherine's boarding house when in Mahonville. Pastor Fry hauled tight on the reins and the lathered horse slid to a stop in a cloud of dust and flying gravel, and danced nervously as the rider jumped from the saddle. The ground-hitched animal was blowing hard. Catherine had never seen Paul shaken by anything or anyone in the rough Colorado mining town down the road from her home, but Paul's eyes were dark with concern, his mouth thin-lipped in an unaccustomed frown. He walked quickly to where Catherine stood.

"Paul," Catherine said as she dropped the wet sheet onto

her basket of dry clothes, "what's the matter? Did something happen to James?"

"No, your boy's in school I'm sure. It's Dan," the Pastor said, placing his hands on Catherine's shoulders and watching her every reaction. "He's been shot."

Suddenly her knees weakened as Catherine struggled to remain calm in spite of a rising sense of dread. Dan Wagner was the only long-term paying boarder she had these days, and while the dollars were few it was enough for a frugal woman to keep the wolf away from the door. But more than that, the young man from Texas was a good friend to both Catherine, a widow for several years, and her son James. Dan and Catherine shared a passion for reading and whiled away many hours in comfortable conversation. "Is it bad?"

"I'm afraid he's dead, Catherine."

"But"––tears welled in her dark blue eyes—"he left here only an hour ago." She leaned against Pastor Fry's chest and squeezed her eyes closed, fighting back the grief rising in her heart.

"The boys took him to old man Jenkins's funeral parlor," the Pastor said, holding her awkwardly. He patted her roughly on the back. A comforter to many people up and down the valley, the preacher still found it hard to know what he should say. "They'll be along directly. We got some talking to do. Why don't you lie down whilst I make us some coffee?"

Soon several of Dan's closest friends gathered at Catherine's place. Roughly dressed men accustomed to the hard work of wresting a living from an unyielding land and no strangers to death, they stood apart from the house. Some neighbor ladies brought food and then sat quietly; it was a traditional part of grieving that came from the South, and in Mahonville it offered comfort where words failed. The boy James came home from school, paled upon hearing the news, then fearfully stayed close to his mother. Hours passed slowly while the men stood around the dooryard in the washed-out sunshine of a late August afternoon. One man offered a bag of makings for the cigarette smokers as others passed a plug of chewing tobacco around. The men spoke in subdued voices. Butter Pegram, a stage driver, seemed to alternate between fierce anger and grief as he raised his voice to make a point. He was the most agitated of the men; he frequently placed a hand on the butt of the pistol he had stuck in his belt, as if to punctuate his speech. Skinny Morris, the stage station cook, seemed to be trying to calm Butter, patting and clucking like an old woman trying to gentle an agitated child. When Catherine came out to talk with them, hats were doffed and the men, mostly rough Westerners, put out their smokes or palmed their chaws and cleaned up their talk to listen respectfully.

After thanking the men for coming to help and comfort her, she scanned the faces before her, and said, "I have some of Dan's old letters. I think we should send a telegram to his father. Even though they were not close, I'm sure he'd want to know."

"Yes'm," Butter volunteered, "I'll get it done day after tomorry when I make the run to Canon City."

"Thank you, Butter," Catherine said, her voice breaking, "Now, about the funeral costs . . ."

"We've all decided to pitch in, Miss Catherine," a man said. Catherine had never seen him before today when he rode in with Butter. "We think it's the right thing to do."

All Catherine could do was smile weakly through her tears. Turning so no one could see the fresh tears that were starting to fall down her cheeks, she made her way through the men as they again quietly whispered among themselves. All knew that a good man had crossed over on this day.

Two weeks later nine strangers, most nearly six-feet tall, squeezed shoulder-to-shoulder onto the three seats of a shiny new, red lacquered six-mule Concord coach with yellow wheels and black trim. The six passengers sitting in the front and middle seats facing each other were forced to interlock their legs in the cramped space that had barely enough room for ten of their twelve legs. Several of the men exchanged good-natured banter, excited about the trip and the prospects that awaited them across the mountains. They noticed the tall man, the man who didn't talk but sat apart from them by the black-leather-curtained window on the left side of the rear seat; their eyes cut quickly away when his cool gaze fell upon them. There was precious little room yet no one crowded him. There was a sense of danger about the quiet one, as if something barely concealed just below the surface gave off warning signals. Studying each of the other passengers in turn, the tall man saw no threat from any of them so he relaxed ever so slightly and thought of the here and now, concluded he was in for a sight of discomfort on the stage, and accepted it. One hand rested on his left knee where deep soreness called to mind a vicious kick delivered by a pack mule in the days when he rode the dry, harsh hills and plains of Texas west of Austin and San Antonio. His strong fingers rubbed the knee hard. Soon it would begin to ache and burn deep inside like a sore tooth if the man sat unmoving too long. He frowned at the thought.

A well-dressed dude, probably an Eastern gambler come out to the camps to relieve miners and cowboys of their hard-earned pokes, sat facing the rear on the middle of the front seat. He pulled out a cigar and with a flourish began the small ceremony of sniffing it, clipping the tapered end with a small knife. That done, he rooted in his vest pocket for a Lucifer.

"Don't light that thing in here, mister, we'll choke to death," someone protested.

Several passengers murmured agreement. Ignoring their protests and with no regard for the comfort of the rest of the passengers, the gambler struck the match and puffed billows of foul smoke into the closed cabin of the coach. With a condescending look he made it very clear he held no esteem for the riffraff he regarded as his travel companions.

"You need to learn some manners," the tall man suddenly said, half-rising from his seat to lean forward across the middle row. One long arm stretched as quickly as a striking rattlesnake to the smoker and grabbed the cigar from the gambler's mouth. The tall man sat down again, opened the curtain and threw the cigar out the window, then crossed his legs and rubbed his knee as if nothing had happened.

"Here," the gambler protested, "you can't—"

The gambler's voice died as he took a closer look at the man across from him on the back row. What he saw was Tilman Wagner, "Long" Tilman to his friends because he stood a shade over six-foot-three in his socks; a lean but wide-shouldered man, with gun butts bulging at his hips under the linen duster he wore. Dark eyes set off by permanent crow's feet stared out under a high-crowned hat, from a tanned face that had weathered hard from years under a relentless sun. The hand that removed the cigar was rough and calloused. Star boots told the gambler the man across from him was one of those he'd heard about in Kansas City, the kind of man, they said, who'd as soon kill you as look at you. Everybody, he was told, hated Texans. If the gambler gave any thought to using that hide-away gun he had up his ruffled sleeve, he decided he'd live a much longer and healthier life if he put such a foolish notion to rest, and the sooner the better. Muttering quietly, the gambler pulled from his coat pocket a pewter flask with his initials etched with grand flourishes in the metal, and studiously avoided the guffaws and amused looks from the other passengers as he began to drink himself to sleep.

Uncomfortable as the passengers were, they were made to suffer by the Barlow and Sanderson ticket agent back at the station, who had insisted that it was company policy that there was always room for one more. Lucky for them none of the other travelers waiting in Canon City were in such a hurry that they wanted to shoehorn into the cab, or worse, endure the long night clinging precariously to the top of the stage. The miles stretched before the stage in the coming darkness, so Tilman closed his eyes, only to be jarred by deep ruts in the road. He could feel the stage slow as the teams pulled up steep grades, and then rush down the other side to gather speed for the next hill. The man on Tilman's right, dressed in a checked suit and wearing a bowler hat, rummaged inside the Gladstone bag he cradled in his lap.

"Care for a taste of forty-rod?" he said as he offered Tilman a pint bottle of evil-smelling whiskey he'd fished out of the bag. "One drink of this," he laughed at his own joke, "and you'll stagger forty rods before you fall!"

"No, thanks, I'll pass." The color reminded Tilman of the tannin-saturated water in the Chickahominy River swamps east of Richmond, Virginia. He'd served in a hard-drinking army, drank his share, but never got to the point where he depended on it, needed it to get through a day—or a night. It slowed his reflexes, and in his line of work that was a sure ticket to an early grave. Tilman was not a temperance man; a drink now and again would do a body good, but some of the stuff that passed for whiskey on the frontier could peel paint off a wall. Grown men gagged when they swallowed some of the worst of it.

Several of the other travelers accepted, passed the bottle around with muttered comments of "Down the hatch," or "Your health," and even one "Skol," from a big square-looking tow-headed fellow who upended the bottle and drained the last of the whiskey and smacked his lips with relish. The empty bottle was tossed out the window, and the curtains were drawn and tied in a vain attempt at keeping out the road dust.

The whiskey talk soon died, each traveler left to face whatever night thoughts or fears that came with the darkness, some lulled to fitful, restless sleep. Were they dreamers, out to strike it rich in the gold and silver boomtowns of

Colorado? Or maybe they were running away from something, like a mortgage, a nagging shrew of a wife and a houseful of young 'uns, or the law back East. Could be one of them was running *toward* something. Tilman was in no mood for conversation to find out. With a will of its own, his right hand reached to his breast pocket to check for the wrinkled piece of paper that lay upon his heart like the weight of the world. Of course it was still there.

The road out of town towards the western valleys had passed the forbidding granite walls of the new state penitentiary, and then climbed higher to snake through some red rock country, hogback ridges tilted and jagged with ominous shadows. After a time the road passed by a town called Buckskin Joe, then came down to the Arkansas River just west of the Royal Gorge where new railroad track was being laid. Tilman had heard talk in the bar of Boyd's Canon City Hotel that armed men built little rock forts in the gorge to protect the work gangs, like the breastworks he'd seen Union soldiers throw up at Gettysburg during the war. There had been a lot of talk about the chance of a shooting war any time now between different railroad factions in the rush to be first to lay track into the boomtowns to corner the shipping trade. Talk had it too that Bat Masterson was leading a gang of toughs sided with one of the railroads. Tilman decided it was best to fight shy of Bat and that crowd, as railroad troubles were no concern of his. He had troubles of his own, and right now, they were all that mattered.

It was a poor stage and freight road—corduroyed in places—which followed along the south bank of the river close to fifty miles through the mountains to the town of South Arkansas. Rocks fallen onto the road from the steep mountain sides were a constant danger to stages, but with only the weak light of two kerosene lanterns hung on the box to see by on this moonless evening the driver whipped the three spans of what must have been green-broke mules as if it were broad daylight. Salida, as some called South

Arkansas, was at the lower end of a wide valley, and Tilman's destination lay maybe twenty-five or thirty miles up that valley, a boomtown called Mahonville.

Many a long ride, trailing rustlers and holdup men, Comanche raiders and Mexican bandits on the Texas frontier had taught Tilman that a man grabs sleep when he can, so he managed some shuteye on the stage. Still, with stops to change out the teams at Texas Creek, Cotopaxi, and Calcite, sleep was never long, and he felt mighty rough by morning. Sporting a three-day beard, and with yellow dust from the road gritty in his mouth, Tilman had an idea that something had crawled into his clothes with him and died. In his forty-odd years he'd traveled worse roads, but never with a reason like this. Tilman's only son was dead and buried in the mountains north of here, and he was bound to find the man or men who killed him. The telegram that started Tilman on this journey was folded in his pocket, but he knew the words by heart. He had only to close his eyes and in his mind the telegram appeared as it did the first time he slit the seal of the delivery envelope with his pocketknife and pulled the folded paper out.

American Rapid Telegraph Company
of San Antonio
Telegram

August 25, 1879
Mister Tilman Wagner
Gunter Hotel
San Antonio, Texas

Dan Wagner murdered yesterday.
Signed: A friend in Chaffee County Colorado

Who was the friend? Tilman knew nobody in Chaffee County. Clearly whoever it was wanted Tilman to come there. Why? Was Dan involved in some sort of trouble? His son was murdered. Tilman knew there was only one way to settle a thing like this. He'd have to find out what really happened and then he'd get the man responsible. Or men. *Lei fuego,* the Mexicans called it, the justice of fire, dealt according to the ways of the Texas frontier, he thought coldly. Tilman would be the dealer in this game.

Chapter Two

The morning sun had just climbed above the rim of the eastern mountains, flooding the valley with warm golden light, when the coach rocked and swayed around a curve before plunging once again into shadows where the road went into the town at the south end of the valley. Off to the right Tilman could see a bend in the Arkansas River, narrow here, clear and cold looking in the early morning light. If he wasn't so full of sorrow and hate Tilman might have been able to enjoy the beauty of the shallow, ice-blue water as it rushed and tumbled over rocks in the riverbed along the side of the dusty road. Men were camped out on a gravel bar by the far bank, some stirring about smoky cook fires in front of white canvas tents while inside, as Tilman could see through open flies, others still slept. Everywhere there were piles of raw earth where hopeful miners had dug prospect holes into the hills on both sides of the river, ever hopeful for the big strike and easy riches that would surely follow. Some men were living in rough dugouts cut into the steep hills, with nothing but log and branch roofs to protect them from the elements. There were but few above-ground, slab-sided shanties. It was a hard life and only a handful of men were really cut out for this and would stick it out.

Up on the coach box, the express guard had been grumbling and swearing since Tilman woke up, but that ended when the stage driver sounded his bugle, announcing their arrival at Bales' station. The horn was a signal to the wranglers to bring out fresh teams and for the station cook to lay out the grub, but for any old soldiers it brought back memories of their days in the Army.

The coach wheeled into the station yard in a cloud of dust, sending a flock of chickens squawking and flapping out of the way as the stage came to a halt. When he thought about fresh eggs, beef and biscuits, and scalding hot coffee, Tilman's stomach rumbled.

"Folks, better have a stretch an' a bait o' breakfast while Miss Cleora's servin' it up," the driver called down from the box. "We'll be pullin' out directly." Before Tilman could get inside, the driver climbed down, pulled off a pair of fine silk gloves, and stepped alongside him and spoke so no one else would hear. "Reckon I could have a word with you, mister?"

"Long as you don't keep me from my coffee, I'm listening."

"Spurgeon, my shotgun, just quit on me. Said he ain't-a-goin' to Mahonville nor Granite. He's scairt o' that Granite Gang, and says there's just too much meanness in them towns to suit his tastes."

"Well, my coffee's getting cold."

"I see'd you back at Canon City. You're what they call a *tejano*, ain't you? You got th' look of a man's been over th' mountain an' rode th' river. I'd say you'd worn a badge somewhere back down th' trail an' you don't look to scare easy." He rolled his chaw and spat a brown stream of tobacco juice into the dust of the yard. "I need a man to ride express guard up on th' box. Th' comp'ny'll pay you, an' I'd be grateful for th' help."

Tilman thought about squeezing back in the coach when he noticed a couple of fancy gamblers waiting to board for a new boomtown further up the line called California Gulch. Though two of their number would be leaving the stage here, these two would take their places. The smell of sweet cologne drifted to where he was standing, and the pomade on one of the slicked-up, gussied-up gamblers reminded Tilman too much of a gunslinger that almost put him under before Tilman got the drop on him down in Laredo. They made up his mind. "Seems like sitting up top, even holding that express gun, might be better than being inside that coach. So, all right, I'll do it."

"Much obliged, mister, an' I'll not keep you from y' grub no longer." The driver nodded his head toward the station door and grinned, "Miss Bales'll whup me if I don't give folks time t' eat."

Tilman had time to finish a second cup of black, scalding hot coffee served up by the rather portly station keeper's daughter when the call came that the new teams were hitched and for the passengers going north to load up. As he stepped out onto the porch, the driver met Tilman there and handed him a sawed-off American Arms 12-gauge shotgun, the breech already open, and a cloth bag of about a dozen shells. By way of introduction, he said, "Folks call me Butter. Let's get a-goin'." Tilman drew two shells from the bag and chambered the double-ought buckshot, snapped the breech closed, and eared the hammers to half cock.

Turning to mount the coach box Tilman looked straight into the face of the devil himself. He felt a sudden, sick sense of dread in his gut, the kind he always got when it came down to someone burning powder in his direction. Not fear, not after all this time, but more like a memory of the stunning shock of a bullet, and what pain follows. A man Tilman hadn't seen before—where did he come from?—was leaning against a post on the station porch, his mouth drawn in a sneering half-smile. Under a fancy *sombrero* tilted back on his head were coal-black eyes, glittering brightly alert, but cold as a grave. There was a tension about the way he held his right hand near a reverse-holstered pistol worn high on his left hip, a short *vaquero* jacket, expensive doeskin

with embroidered lapels, shifted just so to keep it from inter-
fering with his draw. He'd slipped the hammer thong and
was ready for hot work. This was a truly dangerous man.
Tilman had seen his type before. A man notices things about
people if he wants to stay alive. Out here it didn't pay to look
a man straight in the eyes for some in the West take that as a
challenge from a stranger. Many a shootout has started for
nothing more than that. Why did Tilman have the feeling the
man was waiting for him? One look. That was all.

Well, friend, Tilman thought, if you want to open the ball,
then I'll call the tune. Returning the *pistolero*'s stare, Tilman
settled on the left side of the bench seat, the shotgun's muzzle just happening to point at the gunman's big silver belt
buckle. The man's eyes narrowed when he heard the unmistakable sound as Tilman thumbed the shotgun's hammers to
full cock. The business end of that express gun—cut down
for a wide shot pattern—gave any man an edge up close like
this. Tilman saw the man's gun hand ease down and away
from the butt of that pistol. A shotgun up close leaves an
ugly wound, and whatever that Mexican had in mind, the
game was over for now.

Butter released the brake, spoke to the team, and the stage
pulled out of the station yard. The waiting man never moved,
but the sneer had been replaced by a measured interest, a
respectful acknowledgement of a dangerous opponent, as
his eyes held Tilman's until the stage passed on up the road.
Easing the hammers back to half cock, relief eased Tilman's
hard face.

Passing through the small settlement of South Arkansas,
bustling with life now that the railroad was coming, the stage
traveled out into open country close to the river on the eastern side of the valley, and Tilman had a chance to watch
Butter at work. The driver was a small man, wiry and quick.
Wrinkles from years of outdoor living and driving the stage
through sun and snow had worn lines in which the story of
his life could be read. Butter's hair was nearly all gone

except for a small piece that he braided with a colorful scrap of ribbon. His scalp shone in the morning sun when he took off his dusty hat to wipe the sweat from his brow. Anyone could tell he knew how to handle a team by the easy way he held the ribbons, his hands comfortably in his lap, controlling the mules with subtle fingers while hardly moving his hands.

"Why are you wearing those silk gloves?" Tilman asked.

"So I can get a 'feel' for the ribbons," Butter replied. "Heavy work gloves won't do."

"Doesn't it get pretty cold up here come winter? Don't you wear something warmer?"

"Well sir, cold or not, a driver's got to feel th' reins. You'll see good drivers up here who've lost fingers to frostbite. It's part of the job."

His mules were eager for a good run, and Butter let 'em go. The driver's whip never left its holder. Butter, now he was a talker. "Reckon you've not been to Mahonville before. She's a boomin' town, an' a feller'd best go heeled, as I see you do." Butter'd watched when Tilman shifted the faded duster and uncovered a belted Colt .45 as the men climbed aboard the box. Butter had missed none of the exchange between Tilman and the man on the porch.

"Butter, who was that man back there at the station?"

"Never see'd him, but know'd th' type. Mexican *pistolero*. Earn's a livin' with a gun I reckon, an' on the prod. He was a-sizin' you up," Butter grinned, "an' may be he's yore welcomin' committee."

Was that the way it was to be in Mahonville? Tilman laid the shotgun across his knees, and nodded. They rode without conversation. For several miles the only sounds were the wooden wheels turning, iron tires on gravel, the drumming of hooves, and the mules snorting dust from their nostrils. The road here was a good one, and the stage made good time. After crossing the river twice the road climbed towards the middle of the valley. Off to the right were groups of men and mule teams making the grade for the new railroad down on the flats, the tracklayers pushing hard behind them. An engine, white billows of steam escaping in the cool air, backed a couple of flat cars loaded with rails and ties to keep up with the work gangs. They passed from sight as the stage climbed higher. Tilman had lived most of his life down around sea level and noticed his breath came harder in the thinner air.

Looking around the valley Tilman saw plenty of grass and water, good cattle country, a good place for a man to settle his family. Then he remembered, his anger rising, that he no longer had a family. "Let it go," he muttered.

Butter tilted his head back and squinted out from under the brim of his hat. "Who you talkin' to?"

"Sorry, Butter. I was thinking out loud, I reckon," Tilman replied. He changed the subject. "I'd heard how high it was up here but I didn't think it would make me sound like a wheezy old man, just taking a breath." Butter nodded as he scratched his shiny scalp. Tilman took the cue, "Mind if I ask how you came by that name?"

"When I was just a young 'un," he said as he grinned a gap-toothed smile, "I put butter on near 'bout ever' thing Ma put on my plate. She swore I kep' her wore out a-churnin' butter, so naturally Pa put me to doin' the churnin'. Said that way she could mind her other chores. I still like it, 'specially sprinkled with a tad o' salt on a hot biscuit, but I don't churn no more." He continued. "An' you, what do folks call you?"

Tilman had a feeling his questions had given Butter the opening he'd been waiting for, a chance to find out what brought him here, so far from Texas.

"Tilman Wagner." Tilman watched Butter's face, but the eyes revealed nothing.

"Pleased to meet you, Mister Wagner," was all Butter said. Either the name meant nothing, Tilman thought, or Butter would be a hard man to read in a poker game.

The road passed by more prospect holes cut into the low hills, and several working mines came into view.

"Eastern fellers, mostly." Butter pointed with a nod of his head toward several poorly made dugouts carved into the sloping hills near the A-frame hoist over a mine entrance. "Never wintered this high. They'll be mighty cold come full winter." He laughed. "Guess you Texas boys are the same!"

Catherine stood by her husband's grave, marveling at the solitude of the place. That's late husband, she reminded herself. With a start she realized she couldn't remember clearly what Henry had looked like. How could that be? They'd been married for four years before James was born. Henry had been a good man who'd dreamed of building the kind of dairy herd in Colorado that he'd had back on the family farm near Lancaster, Pennsylvania. But things just never seemed to work out for him. He'd try, but something always got in the way. A grizzly bear had killed his prize bull soon after they arrived here. Folks had said it was a fluke, that most grizzlies had been hunted out many years ago. An early fall blizzard had decimated Henry's herd of cows, for Pennsylvania stock couldn't seem to adapt to the harsh, high mountain valley climate of Colorado. People said a storm that early in the fall was a freak, but his cows were dead, freak storm or not. Henry's horse had slipped on muddy ground and fallen on him and broken Henry's right thigh. He lay out in the foothills all night until someone found him the next day. An infection had set in where a jagged end of bone had come through the skin and Henry died soon after, screaming through a delirium of fevers so bad that the doctor told her the amount of laudanum it would take to kill her husband's pain would also kill him. A frightened James hid out in the barn—his hands pressed against his ears—and wouldn't come in the house to see his father. As if to add insult to the poor man's injury, her memory of him had almost faded away. Soon there'd be nothing left of Henry

but their only child, James, and even he took after her side
of the family.

She looked across the cemetery at a new grave. It was
Dan's. She'd brought flowers for his grave. Odd, she thought,
I remember a friend but can't remember my husband.

How could Dan be dead? Why him? He'd harmed no one,
and was a hard working, gentle young man with a kind word
for all. When her two other boarders suddenly took other
lodging, Dan was the one to stay. James seemed to come out
of his shell around Dan. But since Dan's death, her son was
quiet, and all the boy's laughter and fun had gone as well.
Catherine stood and walked to the new grave, removed the
dead flowers left from her last visit, and laid a bright bou-
quet on the raw earth mound. She wondered if Dan's father
had received the telegram. Would he come? Butter didn't
think so. According to Dan, his father was a hard man who
never showed a father's love. Was he still that way or had
time eased his pain and gentled him? She decided that any
man like that would never be gentled, nor would he ever
travel such a great distance just to visit the grave of the son
he hardly knew. What did she expect, anyway? Her part in
this business was done. Dan was just a boarder. But what if
he had been older? Might he have been more? Catherine
remembered an evening when Dan read to her haunting lines
written by a poet, John Greenleaf Whittier: *For of all sad
words of tongue and pen, the saddest are these: 'It might
have been.'*

*No sense in crying over what might have been, Catherine
my girl,* she thought as she stood, brushing the seat of her skirt
while tucking a long wisp of flyaway reddish-gold hair behind
her ear. To be practical, and she was a practical woman, what
was she to do? Bill Ward would know. Catherine untied her
mare and climbed into the hack, took up the reins and settled
into the seat. She pulled a woolen lap blanket over her legs.
She decided she'd ask Bill next time he came calling.

*   *   *

Tilman had never been to the mountains of Colorado and knew he'd have to learn the way of things quickly if he was to do what he must. The stage was traveling into the upper Arkansas Valley. Butter explained that to the west lay the Sawatch Range and the continental divide, with peaks there reaching above fourteen thousand feet. The peaks were snow-capped already even though it was only September. Over to the east was the Mosquito Range, lower in elevation but no less rugged and with barren tops above the tree line as well.

They crossed land carved by crystal-clear rivers that had rushed down from the peaks to the west in some cold, distant past when glaciers in these mountains melted, leaving odd, U-shaped valleys that now channeled the spring runoff. Some of the old riverbeds, like the one Butter called Brown's Creek, cut fifty feet or more down into the outwash plain and were nearly half a mile wide, yet the bottoms were flat. Here, like most places out west, the lines drawn by watercourses were marked everywhere by tall, majestic cottonwood trees, some fifty feet tall, their leaves already turned brilliant yellow by frost. These days the meandering streams in the old beds were shallow and only a few feet wide, but the many washes sloping down across the path reaching for the Arkansas kept the stage going up and down.

"She weren't no town a'tall till a year or so back, not even durin' the Lake County War of '75 or '76," Butter shouted, "but when the railroad looked like it was a-comin' up the valley, why, she boomed. Reckon there's two, three dozen saloons, a couple o' barrels with a plank between 'em for a bar, servin' pizen for whiskey all day an' all night long. There's a store or two, one 'r two hotels an' a couple of places where a man can get a meal, twenny-five cent. Why, one o' them eatin' places, run by a honest man an' his woman, serves up pies an' sinkers an' such truck," he smiled, "an' I dearly love 'em."

"Yes sir, so do I," Tilman agreed as they rumbled along.

Encouraged by a good listener, Butter kept right on talking. Suited Tilman, for he learned from folks who naturally like to talk. Tilman studied the layout of the valley.

"Mean don't begin to describe Mahonville," Butter snorted, "worser'n California Gulch, I'll say. Such a set of hard-cases I've never seen. You name it mister, an' they're there: Swells, miners, railroaders, tramps, two-bit swindlers, thieves, pickpockets, fast women, an' all. Murder ain't uncommon. They say so far this year ten men was buried before one finally died natural."

The road moved west, further away from the river, and climbed up onto an old outwash plain that formed an apron at the foot of the mountains. They crossed rangeland with good, knee-high grass where fat cattle grazed, brought down from their high pastures ahead of winter's promised storms. The clear morning air, warm in the bright sunshine, shimmered as the sky filled with white puffy clouds, like it nearly always did this time of year down in Texas. This part of Colorado was prosperous country, and Tilman read several different brands on the stock they passed. Somebody was doing well here.

Butter continued. "Law can't handle 'em all. Regulators from the vigilance committee run off one judge a year or so back, and shot another dead in his courthouse. Folks tell me the new judge give up," he laughed, "an' they's so many cases on the docket he just fines 'em ten dollars, murderers 'n all, an' turns 'em loose."

"Oh, they's good folk here," Butter went on, "mostly farmers and ranchers who was here before ever there was a town. Why, we even got ourselves a travelin' preacher comes around on snowshoes in winter, an' some Papist folks is tryin' to start a real church!"

Tilman found it hard to imagine a church in such a wild and remote place. "Butter, who runs this town?"

"You ain't a greenhorn, but I'll tell you this. You figger on hornin' in," he glanced sidewise at Tilman, "then you'll be up agin' couple fellers got things sewed up tighter 'n Dick's hatband. If I was you I'd just pass on through."

No names. Butter seemed to lose interest in conversation as the road dropped down to a shallow ford across Chalk Creek. Butter slowed the mules, eased the brake with his right foot to take the ford slowly so's not to splash cold water on the passengers. Butter figured the climb up the other side would be a good place for any holdup men to wait where there was a thick stand of tall cottonwood trees. Out of habit Tilman once again checked the loads in the shotgun. Butter noticed and nodded, but they reached the top of the grade on the other side safely then began to pick up the pace. They soon passed by the scattered buildings of the little settlement of Nathrop in a cloud of dust. As the stage rushed by the town workers were hammering and sawing on the nearly completed station for Wall and Witter's new fast line stagecoaches. Looked like Tilman had earned a free passage on this leg of the trip. Relieved, Tilman let the hammers down on the shotgun and thought once again about the unknowns he would face in Mahonville.

Chapter Three

The stage road straightened toward the center of town where the Mahon family established the original stage station. At first glance, it wasn't what Tilman had expected. The settlement that had grown up around the station was naturally called Mahonville. This was the station where Tilman's son Dan was supposed to work.

The stage and freight road continued on out of town to follow the river north towards Granite and then California Gulch up to the far end of the valley. As the stage pulled up at Mahon's station, the main street headed west to climb the slope towards some mines and logging camps on Cottonwood Creek, and then continued on towards Tin Cup, another boomtown across the pass. The muffled boom of a blast of Giant powder set off by the graders to break through granite boulders echoed through the town. The blast seemed lost in the raucous noise of Mahonville.

It'd been several years since Tilman had seen such a raw looking place. Dusty streets were crowded with men coming and going, jostling each other on the boardwalks. A mule brayed and several sorry-looking black dogs barked at a line of freight wagons strung along the street out to the north, while the swearing and shouting of the bullwhackers added to the general confusion of noise and activity on the street. Every bullwhacker anywhere else in the world could cuss a blue streak, and these were no different. Saloons went full blast, horses stood three-legged at hitching rails out front of several of them. A brewery wagon loaded with huge kegs advertising "Stumpf's Pueblo Lager" beer creaked down the street to make a delivery. There were shouts and men's rough laughter inside the bars. Along a row of unpainted, raw wood buildings that crowded the dusty street, the tin-panny sound of a piano came from the "New York Music Hall" where a sign invited one and all to MEET OUR NEW HOST-ESSES. A "French Dancing Academy" two stories tall stood alongside the "Grand Theatre." It didn't look too grand. Across the street several worn-looking, hard women stood in the open doors to their cribs, dead eyes following the stage. Their nightclothes advertised they were already open for business, and their obscene calls to any man who passed by promised "a good time." Old before their time, most used laudanum to ease the daily pain of living. The women lent a grim air to the town's welcome. The sudden sharp pop of pistol shots rang out but nobody seemed to take any notice. A drunk celebrating? Somebody settling a score? It seemed to Tilman that Butter was right about this town.

At the stage station, Tilman left the shotgun and shells on the seat and jumped down to stretch and collect his gear. While the teams were being changed, Butter showed Tilman a storeroom out back where he could bunk, compliments of the company for being express rider, and pointed out Mister Morris, the cook, who stood in the kitchen door and wiped his hands on an apron stained by preparations for the noon meal. Butter then climbed aboard the coach and pulled out for Granite. One of the company wranglers, a pale hatless young man wearing bib overalls, rubber stable boots and a grim expression sat on the box alongside Butter to ride shot-gun for the next leg.

The storeroom didn't look like much. He'd have to be

careful of the low ceiling—the nickname "Long" fit Tilman well. In one corner was a bed of sorts, rope for springs with a thin but clean straw tick mattress, and to complete the furnishings there was a rough table and a sapling chair. Nothing fancy, Tilman decided; it would suit one of those Spartan soldiers he had read about. Dropping his gear, Tilman stepped outside on a wooden sidewalk to look around. Look hard as he might, he didn't see any beauty in this place. He had to find answers, to learn the truth, for there was an open account to be settled. Tilman would either bring his son's killer to justice or take vengeance. Life had worn any possible softness out of Long Tilman. He was known as an honest man of strongly held principles. But where he once saw everything as right or wrong, good or bad, with no possible shades in between, experience had tempered his views, somewhat. However, he was a man who would back water for no one. He was not a religious man and certainly couldn't quote from the Book, but Tilman's belief in an eye for an eye was not far off from the fiery teachings of the Old Testament. Once crossed, Tilman would not rest until somebody's account was paid in full.

Somebody'll pay, he thought.

Sarah, his boy's ma, wouldn't like that. When he was back from the war, made a hard case by years of fighting and killing for a lost cause, Tilman saw in her eyes the hurt his rough ways caused. She was always trying to tame him. "You got to learn to let it go and forgive," she'd say. "It will eat you up inside otherwise." Tilman thought he did, for a while. Made him a churchgoer. Sarah'd laugh and call Tilman a "pew Christian," warming the pew of a Sunday, and forgetting the teaching till the next Sunday.

The Texas frontier west of Austin, out there around Packsaddle Mountain on the Colorado River, was no place for her gentle ways. Had Tilman known how bad it was, he'd have stayed in North Carolina instead of emigrating with those other ex-Confederates. Texas Rangers had kept the

Indians and renegades on the run before the Civil War, but when the carpetbaggers came to Texas after the war, one of the first things they did was disband the Rangers as a threat to their government. The carpetbaggers set up their own state police force, and a sorrier bunch never claimed to keep the peace. Mostly they were afraid to leave the protection of a town, and they'd steal anything come to hand as quick as the worst two-bit thief. Even Davidson, their chief, the so-called Adjutant General of Texas, was no better, for he left town in the middle of the night with near thirty-five thousand dollars of public money!

Tilman tried to make the best of it. About that time, with his son Dan, he decided he'd throw in with John Chisum and make a cattle drive. Chisum planned to move six or seven hundred head from his home at Paris, Texas, all the way to Fort Sumner, New Mexico, and offered several small ranchers a chance to earn some working capital to improve their spreads. Tilman had met Chisum when he first arrived in Texas. Chisum had a reputation as a man fair in his dealings with others, one who paid his debts, a man whose distaste for violence made him stand out from the carpetbagger crowd around Austin in those days. Chisum was a man born to the land and a natural leader, of only average height but physically strong. Why, when he set out to do a thing it got done! Chisum's features mirrored the wild Texas country he rode every day of his life. Piercing blue-gray eyes in a ruggedly weathered face, his one vanity seemed to be his neatly trimmed but full brown mustache. Sarah saw goodness in the man, prayed over it and felt right about Tilman making the drive.

One day Tilman and the boy were out in the river bottoms rounding up unbranded cattle that'd been let run wild for the war years when three Comanches rode up by the house, probably looking for food. They had caught Sarah outside, her rifle left by the springhouse, and killed her.

Tilman covered his grief with anger. He tracked the

Indians all the way back to the Panhandle cap rock country where he left their bodies to the coyotes, and then Tilman burned their skin lodges with all their blankets and food they'd laid up for the winter. Reckon their squaws, old folks and young'uns had a rough time of it. Tilman never took the time to find them—he was a hardcase, who walked a man's walk, and he was not the kind to hunt down women and children—but he believed the Indian families probably lit out for the reservation at Fort Sill, where the government agent would issue rations and blankets to see them over the winter.

Forgive, Sarah would say.

If Tilman had lived the way she had wanted him to, his life might have been different. But Tilman felt he was too old to change his ways and didn't reckon he'd ever go back to ranching. Somebody'd taken his last link to her away from him, and there was the devil to pay.

If he were to find the killer, he'd need information to start his search. As he never was one to put things off, Tilman started with Skinny Morris, the station cook.

"You know Dan Wagner?" There was no reason to waste time with niceties.

"You the law?" He looked sidewise up at Tilman, his manner cautious.

"Dan was my son. I'm Tilman Wagner."

He looked around, saw no one nearby, took off his apron and rolled it up. "Let's us take a little passear as you boys from Texas like to call a short walk, down yonder by the river. We can talk there."

What kind of a place is this? The cook can't talk out in the open? What or who's got him so buffaloed?

The two men walked down the main street, weaving through crowds of men drawn by the excitement of boom times. There were still more music halls, gambling dens, and saloons, all busy, and then they passed the end of the street and neared the river. Looking back, Tilman guessed there must be thirty or so saloons in that small town. Morris hadn't said much along the way.

"Town's first stamp mill," Morris said, pointing across the river to the right, at a tall, wooden building nearing completion downriver from the town.

The building seemed to grow out of the side of the mountain. Tilman had never been in a mining town before, and Morris must have read the blank look on Tilman's face, for he patiently explained. "The mineral, gold or silver, will be in rock they blast out of the mines. That's the ore. Then they'll bring the rocks down to this place and dump 'em in the top so they'll drop down through two or three sets of stamping machines. Breaks the rock into little pieces, so it's a pretty fine mix by the time it gets to the bottom. Then they'll soak that in some strong chemicals to separate the metal. After that they'll melt the metal and make bars, and Butter'll haul it to Como on the treasure wagon ever' other month till the railroad gets to town. She'll be noisy when she starts."

"'Treasure wagon?'" Tilman had never heard of one of those. "What's that?"

"A stagecoach with iron plate hung on it to stop bullets in a holdup. Around here we use it to haul gold dust and such. When she makes a run, there's two guards inside, and there's three or four outriders too."

Off to the left was a large corral where the company kept its stock, and a smithy. Inside the barn a man stood in the shadows forking hay down from the loft, and what looked like a freight building with an office was in front. A mule-drawn wagon was drawn up to the freight loading dock where a man with wide shoulders and powerful arms was muscling heavy white bags onto a hand truck. When the truck was loaded he'd wheel it through open double doors into the building. He was sweating heavily, grumbling to himself in a monotonous tone as he worked. Inside, a tall man made notes in a tally book as each load was dropped off.

"Howdy, Shorty," Morris called to the freighter, getting only a grunt in return as the man pulled a rag out of his hip pocket and wiped sweat from his eyes.

"That's old Shorty Bain. Folks call him Shorty on account of his temper. He gets mean, sometimes. Hauls ore bags down from a couple of mines up in the hills. We lock 'em up in the company's strongroom to hold 'em till the stamp mill's done. Right now we just hold the high grade, I mean the rich stuff, eighty dollars or so a ton, here."

"High grade." The words brought a grim smile to Tilman's face. Morris seemed a likeable sort. "I've heard that before. When my pap was younger he worked a gold mine for a man up at a place called Gold Hill near home. He'd tell about some of the boys who'd find a chunk of gold and slip it in their lunch pail when the boss wasn't looking. Called it 'high-grading.' "

"Happens here, I've heard," Morris said, "but sort of on a different level. Over in the San Juans a couple of bold fellers last year run a high-gradin' job at a mine an' one night they slipped off with fifty or so burros loaded with high grade ore, mostly pure quartz shot through with gold threads."

"They stole rocks?" Tilman asked.

"Ore," Morris corrected, "and bags of gold dust from the placers. Y'see, after the tally boss checked the bags of high grade in the storage drift up at the mine, then these boys'd switch for some low grade rock they'd hid in another drift. When they'd set aside all they could handle, why, they got the night watchman drunk and made their play. Never did catch 'em," he laughed. "Now, that's what I call high-gradin'."

"Couldn't somebody do that here?"

"I reckon."

"That's the last of 'em, Bill," Shorty called out to the man inside. "Now I'm headed for that bucket o' cold beer you promised."

Tilman heard a response, but couldn't make it out. As Shorty drove off in the wagon, cussing the mules, a man

Tilman guessed to be the one Shorty called Bill came out to close and lock the doors.

Morris didn't speak to this Bill.

The Texan and the cook continued on around to the front and stepped up on the porch by the office, the door padlocked.

"Me and him was a-standin' here," Morris said as they stood outside the station door, "havin' a cup of coffee, waitin' for the treasure stage from Granite, the one hauls the silver bars and gold dust." He pointed with the toe of his well-worn brogan to a dark stain. Three weeks since, Tilman thought as his anger welled up like a cold, vicious thing, yet Dan's blood still showed in the rough-cut pine plank flooring of the porch. Somebody here sowed the wind killing the boy, and Tilman had come as the whirlwind, come to find out the truth about who did it, and make sure that person reaped a whirlwind of justice. "Jus' one shot. Ball hit Dan dead center of his chest. I seen the smoke"—he pointed to a jumble of rounded, gray granite boulders pushing up through a stand of Ponderosa pines across the Arkansas River from where they stood—"up in them rocks yonder."

Tilman knew right off whoever had done the shooting was good at it. Most men when they shoot downhill tend to shoot high, and usually miss with their first shot. He guessed the distance was a good three hundred yards, maybe more, so if the shooter only needed the one shot he knew his business.

"I took Dan by the arm and drug him inside," Morris continued, "but I seen right off it warn't no use, he was done for." He plunged a hand into his pants pocket to withdraw a brass cartridge case. "It's a Sharps Big Fifty," he said as he handed it to Tilman. "I found it after I crossed the river and looked around the rocks where that feller that done it hid." Morris pointed again to a jumble of rocks on the side of the hill. "Found footprints of only one man up there where he waited."

Tilman looked at the rocks where Morris indicated.

"He'd smoked several cigarettes, taken his shot," Morris said, "and walked over a rim to where he'd left his horse.

"Mister Wagner, I got to tell you that the town constable never asked who done it, and the coroner ruled Dan's death a hunting accident. I'm sorry, but that explains a lot about this place. I thought the world of Dan. Butter's th' one sent you th' telegram to San 'tonya. Miz Stone, over to th' roomin' house where Dan stayed, she wanted Butter to do that, an' she made sure a preacher spoke words over Dan when we buried him."

Morris had a lot to say, like he knew all this and had nobody to tell it to. Tilman wondered why this Missus Stone would help? And why hadn't Butter said anything about sending the telegram? Plus, a person doesn't just step in and arrange a funeral, if for no other reason, one costs money. Who paid for it?

"We all anted up for the forty dollars it cost," Morris said, answering Tilman's unasked question.

"I'm much obliged." *Why would they do that?*

A part of Tilman died right there on the porch, yet he'd no tears, not now. Tilman had shed tears long ago. He felt only a cold, mean certainty that somebody would pay up on Dan's account. If there was one thing in this world Tilman had been good at when he was younger, it was tracking down and either killing or bringing back to justice whoever he went after. Dead or alive, made no difference. He knew he was up to doing it one more time, for Dan.

As they walked back up to the stage station, Morris told Tilman all of Dan's belongings were still at the boarding house, and where to find it. As they neared the station, they heard the unmistakable sounds of fast-approaching hooves, and folks on the street were turning to look at the excitement. Tilman and Morris hurried to the corner, saw the stage careening down the middle of the street with Butter, alone on the box, hauling back on the lines, pulling the stage to a dusty halt in the station yard.

Chapter Four

"They got us not more'n four mile out!" shouted Butter, scrambling down from the driver's perch, while wild-eyed, frightened passengers, several with dark splotches of blood on their clothes, spilled out of the coach and disappeared in the crowd of onlookers who pressed close to see what was going on. "Th' Granite Gang was a-waitin' for us at Elephant Rock, an' they shot pore Lon. He's back yonder in th' coach."

"I'll git th' doc," Morris called as he hurried off, "y'all git Lon inside."

Tilman helped Butter lift the groaning boy, for that's what he was, and they laid him on the table inside the station. Butter used his pocketknife to cut open the boy's overalls. The stomach wound, a puffed black hole oozing blood, was low on Lon's belly. Lon's breathing was shallow and fast, and he was cold to the touch, his skin deathly pale. In a pleading whisper he asked for a drink of water. Butter gently pushed a towel from the washstand onto the wound. Tilman took a dipper of water from a bucket in the kitchen and, raising Lon's head with one hand, held the dipper to Lon's mouth. Butter looked at Tilman and his thoughts did not need saying—the boy's going under.

"It was them three from Granite," Butter explained, his voice high and quavering, "same little feller a-leadin' 'em. He never says anything, just shot Lon off the box an' cleaned us out. How come him do that? Lon'd laid down the express gun and weren't a-goin' to try nothin'." The gawking crowd parted at the doorway as Morris and the doc shouldered through and came clumping into the room, their boots loud on the hardwood floor in an otherwise quiet room. Lon opened his eyes and whispered, "Oh, Ma," and died. Butter's eyes got watery, and he swore, bitterly. "Another friend gone under," he growled, as he gently closed Lon's unseeing eyes. The tenderness of Butter's act came as a surprise to Tilman. Almost like a father, Tilman thought.

Was that shot meant for Tilman? Did somebody expect him to still be the express rider or was it pure chance? Why did they kill that boy? Why was this place so mean? To his way of thinking it might be just as well if somebody was to burn down this town of Mahonville and plow the ashes under. Maybe decent folks could start over and do better next time.

"Well folks, 'nother funeral," Butter sighed as he pulled off his jacket and covered Lon's face. "Seems to me like young Lon here don't have no family. He was a-goin' to church regular whenever the preacher-feller passed through here. He's in town now.

"You'd best go find that preacher," Butter told Tilman.

"Okay, I heard you." Tilman's voice was cold. He didn't take to being told what to do.

"Beg pardon, Mister Wagner." Butter stepped back. "I didn't mean no disrespect."

Tilman shook his head. "Let it go . . . I'll find that preacher."

After a little pointing and a lot of head shaking, he was finally directed to a place on the western edge of town across Cottonwood Creek, sheltered among some tall old cottonwood and spruce trees. The afternoon sun behind the trees made them glow a brilliant yellow. Reminded Tilman of Chinese lanterns. It was quiet there in that grove of trees away from the bustle of town, like a restful side yard to the Hell of Mahonville, if there could be such a place. In a grassy area stood a makeshift, open-air altar and beside it a young woman sat on a rough-hewn bench, deep in conversation with a man wearing a faded black suit and a battered straw hat, the kind Tilman had often seen old Preacher Sharp wear back at Marble Falls.

"Excuse me, Reverend." Tilman removed his hat and nodded to the lady. "Ma'am."

"I'm sorry, brother, but I don't recognize your face." The man smiled. "Are you one of the new ones here?"

The smile faded as the preacher sized up the big Texan; his eyes lingered on the worn but obviously well cared for Colt. He knew exactly the kind of man who stood before him, but his eyes questioned why such a man would bother to take the time to talk to a preacher.

"No. And I'm not a church-going man, either. There's a sight of meanness in this world. My wife Sarah went to church, but she was murdered." Why did Tilman tell him that? He owed no man any explanation. "There's been another killing, so I've come now about a boy I believe you know, name was Lon. He's dead. I want you to speak over him."

The preacher assured Tilman he'd take care of Lon. Tilman watched the preacher go explain to the woman, who still sat waiting patiently. Angrily, Tilman turned and walked away from that place to head back toward the town.

As he came to the makeshift footbridge across the fast-flowing creek that cut the path back to the main street, Tilman saw four bigger boys ganged up on a little scrawny one, who had a bloody nose.

"Don't you talk about my mama that way!" the little one sputtered through tears.

"That's enough!" Tilman called out, catching the bullies

by surprise. "Go on home now and let him be!" Anger made his voice louder than he'd intended.

They ran away when Tilman walked toward them, calling taunts of "Crybaby" and "We'll get you," over their shoulders at the little one.

"Come on, boy, let's get you cleaned up." Tilman squatted down by the stream and wet his bandanna in the icy cold, clear water. The boy had been thrown to the ground in the roughhousing, so Tilman brushed some leaves off the back of his shirt, and sat him up on one of the boulders by the stream so he could wipe the blood off the boy's face. Tilman showed the lad how to pinch his nose shut and lean his head back to stop the bleeding. "This is how we used to handle a bloody nose when I was your age. Say, if I hadn't come along just now, I'll bet you were fixing to tear into those boys. Mad as you were, you'd have given them quite a thrashing."

That got a tentative smile as the boy took a deep, shuddering breath and struggled to hold back his tears. "Thank you for helping me," he said, then jumped down from the rock and turned to leave. "I better get home now."

"Those your schoolbooks over yonder?" Tilman pointed to a McGuffey's Speller and another book bundled up with an old leather belt.

"Yes sir." He slung the books over his shoulder, and started up a footpath toward the mountains. He turned and waved.

As Tilman watched him go he remembered when Dan was this age. Some father Dan had; Tilman was never around to be one. Tilman had always put aside his absence, and for justification convinced himself that he had to go to the war, had to move to Texas, and it took time to start up a ranch, didn't it? Tilman was always too busy to take time for his own son. Who had wiped his face, Tilman wondered, and taught him to be a man? He hoped that little boy going up the path yonder had a pa who would take time with him when he got home today. Tilman was almost back into the town when he realized he wasn't angry any more, at least, not for now.

Back home again after she'd taken old Mollie Ahern some fresh bread, Catherine went out to the hen house to gather some eggs when a freight wagon, heading up the road to Cottonwood Pass, stopped and the driver hallooed her. She recognized the driver as Hubert Smalls, a fieldhand who used to help out on the place while her husband was still alive. He sometimes stopped to leave her a sack of flour or coffee or a bag of dry beans and pass on gossip of the town. Hubert stuttered, and Catherine supposed he liked to stop and talk with her because she accepted him without ridiculing his impediment the way some of the townspeople did. Hubert's gift was a small sack of buckwheat flour, and the news about the stage robbery, with yet another young man killed. Catherine talked with Hubert a bit and fetched him a loaf of bread from the batch she'd made the night before, and then waved good-bye. The news did nothing to ease her growing concern about the increasing violence in the town. Returning to the safety of her kitchen, she stood by the sink. She had to do *something*, but what?

The screen door slammed followed by the sound of footsteps in the front hallway and Catherine knew James was home from school. "Go out on the back porch and wash up and come on in the kitchen," she called, "I've made you some sugar cookies."

James slipped into the kitchen and, head down, shyly pulled a three-legged stool out to sit at the corner table. As Catherine turned from the pie safe to place cookies on a saucer in front of James, the boy looked up and smiled at his mother, dried blood on his upper lip and caked around his nostrils.

"James!" Catherine sat on a stool beside the boy and took his shoulders in her hands.

"I'm okay, Mom," he said, shrugging her hands away. "They didn't hurt me. And, look, my hands are clean."

Dipping a dishcloth in a water pail, Catherine washed the boy's face and hands. *They? Boys! Why do boys always get into fights?* "Tell me about it," she said.

"Mom, they were saying things again. I don't like it when they say things about you."

"James, you—"

"Mom, a man helped me."

"What man?"

"I don't know. He was BIG." With wide eyes he exaggerated his voice. "Bigger than Mister Dan, even, and he showed me how to stop my nose from bleeding."

Catherine pulled James into her lap, hugged him, and sat quietly.

"Mom?"

"Yes, James."

"Mom, that man. When he talked he sounded like Mister Dan."

He's here. Catherine knew with certainty. Dan's father was in Mahonville. "Now, you eat and then run along and let me start supper. Mister Ward is coming by for dessert and I want you cleaned up and on good behavior, young man." A warm feeling of anticipation came over her. Not for her caller, Bill Ward, but for a man she'd never met, nor even expected to meet. What would he be like? How did he come to help James? He didn't frighten James, whoever he was. A big man, James said, but gentle enough to help a boy in trouble. Nothing Dan had ever said about his father could be taken to mean the man had one iota of caring in him. To the contrary, he was all rough and harsh, cold even. Maybe it wasn't Dan's father after all. "I wonder," Catherine said aloud.

Chapter Five

The next morning Tilman was ready to begin his search for a place to stay, but first he needed a way to get around. Tilman had known some Texas cowboys down around the Llano country who were so set on working from a saddle they wouldn't lower themselves even to walk across a street. They'd unhitch, climb aboard, amble across and get down on the other side of the street. Tilman was never that bad but the fact was he'd need a horse to get around the valley and see about finding Dan's killer. Morris said the town livery might have some stock worth looking at, so Tilman headed that way. The streets of the town were alive with the comings and goings of people in an amazing variety of shapes, sizes, and dress styles. Most of the new citizens had heard stories of gold nuggets lying in streambeds waiting to be picked up, all drawn by the prospect of sudden, easy riches.

Tilman leaned on a gray and worn fence rail by the livery paddock and looked at the string. The hostler sat reading a dime novel in a chair tilted back on two legs against the barn where he could enjoy the morning sun. He was a lean, grizzled man probably in his early fifties, and he wore a black cloth patch over the socket of his right eye.

"He'p you?" he called out, as he stood and tossed the book into the chair.

"Lookin' for a hoss," Tilman said.

"You that feller rode shotgun for Butter?" he asked as he left his chair, squinting his one good eye. Tilman nodded, and the hostler said, "Morris tol' me you was Dan's pa 'cept he didn't tell me you was seven-foot tall," he chuckled. "Must be that high-crowned hat and them high-heeled boots all you boys from Texas favor. You look like Dan, and danged if he didn't wear the same kind of hat."

"I want folks to know when I'm around."

"I hear some folks know you're here. Some folks might be worried on account of you being here. Word gets around." Stepping up to the rail, he went on, "Up here you'll need a good mountain hoss for what you got t'do." He pointed to a black gelding with a spotted blanket on his rump. "That there paloose's got plenty o' bottom. Bred over in the San Juans, for I bought him off a Ute. He was your boy's horse, an' I reckon now he's your'n. Let's you an' me step in yonder so's we can settle the feed bill," he said as he pointed at the livery office with his chin, "an' I got a bottle."

Inside, away from prying eyes and ears, there was no bottle. "Name's Arch Drye, but folks call me Sheriff, which I was once till I got my eye gouged out in a saloon ruckus in Dodge. Now I ain't no more. But here, I still watch who comes and goes."

He seemed to have something to say, so Tilman asked, "Sheriff, about the time Dan was killed, did you see anything or hear of anybody might have to do with Dan's murder, maybe somebody new in town?"

"There's lots o' new folks passin' through Mahonville, miners an' fancy gamblers an' such, all sorts. Some comes by here, most don't. A body can't 'member 'em all."

"At the South Arkansas station I had a run in with a *pistolero*, hard eyes, probably mean as the devil, big *sombrero*. Have you seen him around?"

"Well sir, I can he'p you there. The man you talk about rode in last night. Seen him around last week too. I hear he's a Mexican scalp hunter. Down in Texas you call 'em bounty hunters. Name of Mendoza, Blas Mendoza, from Silver City way. By reputation he always gets his man, usually brings 'em in tied across a saddle. Lookin' for somebody here, I reckon." Tilman fingered the cartridge case Morris found across the river, the one he now carried in his vest pocket. Buffalo hunters favored that gun for accuracy and for power in knocking down a buffalo. Dan got hit with one of those. Tilman remembered that he had not seen a Sharps near that fellow at South Arkansas. Could it be him? Such guns were common enough in west Texas, and people said King Fischer, that Uvalde cowboy who was known to sometimes cross over the wrong side of the law, fancied such a gun. Unusual for this part of the country where most men make a living digging in the ground rather than hunting game, or other men. It's enough to make a man who used one easier to find, for find him Tilman would unless that fellow lit a shuck and was now out of the country. Did nobody care enough to ask questions? Was this town too much for its peace officers to take the time to look for Dan's killer? Tilman asked as much of the former lawman.

"Don't go to the laws here." He nervously looked around. "The constable's been bought an' you go a-asking the wrong questions, why, you'll just up and disappear like some other fellers done.

"Ever since the Lake County War folks been turnin' up dead; some shot, some hung from a tree. Some folks say the lawmen took a hand in a lot of that business. Back in Feb'wery the commissioners voted to split Lake County to make Chaffee County, this'n here, but that don't change nothin'. Back then it was killin' over water rights, and now it's over just about anything else, but mostly it comes down to gold or silver.

"I thought the world of Dan Wagner," Sheriff continued,

"an' I hated to see him shot down like that. But that man who shot him is a cold-blooded killer, so you be careful."

After hours of useless questioning and listening for information that wasn't to be had, the day was near to being used up before Tilman got up enough courage to go see Dan's grave. He ground-hitched the paloose and found Dan's grave in the cemetery where Morris had said, the mound of soil bare in front of a rough wooden marker with Dan's name carved on it. A single small bunch of flowers lay near the cross, surprisingly fresh white marigolds tied with a bright yellow ribbon. It made Tilman catch his breath. Marigolds were Sarah's favorite flower. Was that just a coincidence? No, he never believed in such. In this world there's a reason for everything, only sometimes it's hard for people to see it. Who put the flowers there? Somebody knew Dan well enough to know about those flowers.

The sun was dipping below the rim of the western mountains and a cold wind gusted down the valley, bending the tall bunch grass and blowing fallen golden aspen leaves among the graves in the gathering dusk. It was quiet there a short distance away from the town. Tilman looked at the clear sky, and at the darkening mountains, and it was not just the coolness of autumn that gave him a chill. His mind was filled with questions. Why did those Comanches happen to come by on a day when he wasn't close to the house? Sarah was the only woman he'd ever loved, and they killed her. Now his only son had been murdered. It looked like anybody he loved was bound to die a hard death. Was there a connection somehow with the rough life he'd led?

"Vengeance is mine!" Tilman remembered the preacher at Marble Falls shouting from the pulpit. Well, in his time, maybe, but right here and now, this was the right time. Tilman was not prepared to wait on the off chance that Dan's killer would be brought to justice by and by.

Tilman had never had a chance to set things right with Dan, tell him how he felt. It was too late, and Tilman wanted justice for the killing, but he wanted to impose that justice, and he wanted it to suit the crime.

His dead wife would never have understood why he was driven to find Dan's killer. Tilman had grieved for Sarah, and then he'd turned away from the faith on which she had based her life. There was no room in Tilman's life for any religion that preached forgiveness. Tilman had become the devil's own. His hate for Comanches had broadened to anybody who rode the owlhoot trail. He left off going to church, and sent Dan to live with a good German family that ran a hotel in Fredericksburg, where the boy grew up seeing Tilman only now and again. Tilman rode south Texas like an avenging angel, facing his men when he killed them, a time or two near being killed himself, giving murderers, horse thieves, *bandidos* and rustlers no quarter, for they would give him none. He was a hard case fighting men as hard as he had become. Difference was, sometimes Tilman wore a badge.

Tilman Wagner was here. She had been right. The man that befriended James had to be Dan's father. Catherine knew he was here because the preacher had stopped by on his way to Granite last night. Catherine twisted a lock of loose hair that was always falling out of the braid that snaked down her lean back. She remembered every detail of the evening, going over it in her mind once more.

"He's here, Catherine." The preacher had sighed as he helped himself to a fourth piece of fried chicken. "This chicken is a sin, Catherine. Nothing should be this good." He paused and wiped his mouth with the dangling end of the napkin he had tucked into his shirt collar, and then continued. "Rode in with Butter's stage yesterday afternoon. He's the one who came to find me to tell me about poor Lon. I hardly got to talk to him though." The pastor stopped, shrugged his shoulders and helped himself to the remaining gravy and another biscuit.

Catherine watched him eat, wondering as usual how he managed to consume half the food on the table, yet never seemed to gain a pound. Pastor Paul Fry traveled all over the mountains though and that accounted for a lot of activity.

"I swear, Catherine," Paul laughed, "that is, if I did swear, you are the best cook this side of Denver."

Catherine smiled, clearing the table. "You had better watch it, Paul. All the ladies know chicken's your favorite food, and I'll bet you say that to everyone who feeds you."

"Next to apple pie, Catherine, next to apple pie and coffee." He pointedly stared at the sideboard and sniffed with exaggerated nose wrinkles at the still warm pie that was resting in the center.

"Aha!" Catherine's son James, helping with the dishes, grinned with childish glee. He'd caught an adult bending the truth. "Pastor Fry. I was over at John Malloy's two weeks ago when you were eating there and I heard you say the same words to his mom, except I believe it was a raisin pie you were talking about."

Feigning surprise with a gruff "Harrumph," the preacher got up and started to help clear the table. "Well, now, James—that is right, you have the advantage of me there. The night in question I believe raisin pie won." He rocked back on his heels and hooked his thumbs in his suspenders, stretched and popped them on his chest. "But tonight, definitely, my choice is apple."

James smiled at the preacher, a favorite friend to the children as well as many adults in the valley. The preacher took an apron from a peg near the back door and deftly tied it on. The old bachelor knew his way around a kitchen. "Here, Catherine. Let me finish. I have to help earn my dinner and you know I can't sing."

James and Paul washed and put away the dinner dishes and then sat down in the parlor where Catherine served them thick slices of pie swimming in thick cream. A short time later, James, ever hopeful of outwitting the brook trout that lived in the clear, cold waters of the fast flowing creek behind the house, went out to check the set hooks he tied to dangle in some quiet eddies, while Catherine and Paul sat on the front porch, he with a second steaming mug of black coffee, knowing that in an hour the sun would set and the cool air would be uncomfortable.

"Are you sure I did the right thing with the telegram?" Catherine nervously redid a thread in a quilt she was working on. "I have no idea what was behind Dan's death but I felt like he would have wanted me to let his father know." She paused, "Although Dan never spoke much about his father, I always felt there were things unresolved between them."

"Hard feelings, the boy once told me," Paul said quietly. Changing the subject, Paul admired the evening sky above the mountain rim that made the most expensive canvas in the world look like child's play. "When you see a sunset like this how can you ever doubt that there is a creator of this world?"

"I agree." Catherine said, recognizing by his change of the subject that Paul didn't want to talk about what she'd done. "But the end of a day makes me realize that our time on this earth is so fleeting."

"But no less important, Catherine." Back on firm, familiar preacher ground, Paul's voice was sure, his manner positive. "Don't you think anything different for a moment."

"Mom. Mom! Pastor Fry! Look what I caught!" James came running up the steps to stand proudly before the adults, a large dark lump in his hands.

"What on earth?"

An indignant frog peered angrily at Catherine through James's muddy hands, struggled free, and hopped off the porch in three giant leaps, vanishing into the evening twilight. The mood broken, Paul soon left for his room and Catherine and James went to finish homework.

Later, after Catherine blew out the lamp and lay in the

quiet before sleep, her doubts returned. She was no surer than before if she had been right to summon Tilman Wagner to find who had killed his son, her friend. This day, her doubt remained.

Chapter Six

Tilman was not one to remain in bed of a morning, so first light found him out of his blankets shivering in the chill, his hat on, quickly pulling on his britches and shirt. He shoved his feet into his boots. Fall in the mountains would take some getting used to. He stepped outside and poured some cold water from a bucket into a wash pan, splashed his face, and dried on a towel hung from a nail. Later, there would be time to get a bath and a shave.

Looking around in the dim light, he could hear the sounds of the shallow river as its waters rushed and splashed against boulders, while up the street the town itself was still quiet, most folks sleeping off last night's excesses. Somewhere nearby a screen door slammed, and footsteps crunched on gravel, followed by the sound of a pump working, then water gushing into a bucket. A dog barked. Somebody stirred around the office cookhouse, so Tilman walked over there and went through the door into the dim front room. There was a fire in the fireplace, popping and spitting as chunks of piñon pine began to burn, the sweet pine incense familiar. A couple of kerosene lamps lit the kitchen where the big Franklin cook range glowed warmly, and a gallon-size coffeepot made of gray graniteware simmered on the range.

The smell of frying bacon and sourdough biscuits fresh out of the oven drew him into the room. Tilman's stomach rumbled. Mister Morris pointed to a shelf lined with china mugs, an invite for Tilman to have a cup of Arbuckle's Best coffee with him. He forked a thick slab of crisp bacon into one of those biscuits and Tilman wolfed that down with the scalding hot coffee and, as it was offered, two more after it. Neither of the men was much to talk early in the morning.

"Much obliged."

"Yessir, Cap'n."

Tilman stepped out to the station corral to find a skim of ice on the water trough; he was glad he wore the old woolen shirt he'd placed in the war bag as an afterthought. Tilman saddled the paloose with Dan's gear and led him out of the barn; the huge animal seemed pretty easy going. Leather creaked as Tilman climbed aboard and seated himself. He saw the horse's ears flatten so got ready, and sure enough the horse humped his back and with a grunting snort crow-hopped around the yard letting Tilman know he was a horse that liked to start his mornings with a little excitement. After they came to an agreement as to who was boss, Tilman started up the main street to ride out, get the lay of the land, then to call on the Widow Stone later. The early morning quiet was gone, and a crowd beginning to gather up where the freight road crossed the main street. As he rode nearer he saw a shoeless man, clad only in his nightshirt, with a flour sack over his head, hanging from a big cottonwood in a vacant lot; so it looked like somebody'd hauled him out of bed during the night, and strung him up. Several men in the crowd were fixing to cut him down while off to one side some hard-eyed gents talked quietly, cutting their eyes at Tilman. No policeman was in sight, so that told a lot about this town. A paper pinned on the dead man's shirt had the words WAS TOLD TO GET OUT scrawled in big letters, and below that, AKANSAS VALLEY COMMITTEE OF VIGILANCE AND SAFETY. He reckoned that's what passed for local justice; Tilman knew it was the same as he'd seen in San Angelo, across the river from Fort Concho. Butter's comments about the meanness of Mahonville came to his mind. *How right you are,* Tilman thought. He rode on, the bright morning sun not able to overcome the grim spectacle of a man's sudden, brutal death.

Was that so different from what Tilman came here to do? He decided he had no intention of bringing a murderer to stand trial in this town, taking a chance with a local jury's excuse for justice. He meant to give no more chance to a killer than Dan had gotten, and then Tilman would be hauling his freight for Texas. Hadn't he always been that way? Well, since he lost Sarah, anyway.

He followed the slightly uphill road west maybe a mile to the place where Cottonwood Creek came out of the mountains. Taking his time, Tilman stopped often to use his field glasses to get an idea about the land around the town. The glasses once belonged to Captain Gantt, his company commander in the old 26th North Carolina. Gantt taught his men to learn as much as possible about the land where they were going to fight—visual reconnaissance, he said. In Tilman's first battle, when the Yankees flanked them early one September morning at Sharpsburg in a smoky cornfield by the north woods, Gantt quickly got his men in defilade. Saved a bunch to fight another day. He also taught young Tilman about staying cool under fire for Gantt himself was a man who seemed to have no nerves. The captain gave Tilman the glasses when he lay dying at Sayler's Creek in Virginia, long years ago.

Across on the north bank of the creek Tilman found the rooming house where Dan had lived, and was pleasantly surprised to find it was actually a small ranch nestled in the tall spruce trees. A freshly painted barn and several outbuildings hid behind a neatly painted two-story home with a white picket fence. A very large climbing red rose bush covered the railing on one side of a comfortable-looking porch. It seemed as though Tilman could smell its sweetness from where he was. It appeared out of place in this valley of death, for that was how Tilman was beginning to think of the Arkansas Valley.

As he watched, a woman came out from the house carrying a large, oval, braided rug on her arm. She hung it over the porch railing and proceeded to stir up a cloud of dust as she beat the rug until there couldn't have been a speck of dust or anything left to mess up her home. Could this be the Widow Stone? In his mind Tilman had envisioned a much older woman, skinny as a rail or one politely called "stout." Maybe this one was a daughter, or maybe hired help. But no one had said anything about a daughter come to think of it. The morning sun seemed to cause the woman's hair to glow as it bounced with each blow to the rug.

She was singing now, and some of the words he could hear ". . . *tell it on the mountain* . . ." were familiar.

He might have known! What was it with some women that they seemed to know every spiritual and hymn by memory that ever was written? Sarah used to sing for hours, going from one song to the next, serenading the countryside in a loud and usually off-key voice. Not that Tilman had minded. He used to like to listen to the joy in her voice, the discordant notes lost in her love for life. Just then the woman turned and went back into the house. The yard seemed strangely quiet.

A boy, maybe eight or ten years old, wearing overalls and a corduroy coat too big for his small frame, watched from the front steps as Tilman rode up, dismounted, and hitched the reins through a post-mounted ring. Steeling himself, he walked through the gate up the gravel path to the house. Before he got to the steps, the boy shot up, running across the wide porch and went inside, and the screen door slammed behind him as he called for his ma. Tilman recognized him. It was the little boy from the fight he broke up the first day he was in town. As he raised a hand to knock on the door, the woman stepped from the front parlor to face him through the screen door. Peering cautiously around her skirts, Tilman could make out the boy, his two solemn blue eyes peering up at him. The boy had a bruise under his left eye. The town bullies played rough with such a little fellow.

"Yes?" she asked.

"Morning ma'am," Tilman said removing his hat. "My name's Tilman Wagner. I believe my son Dan took a room here."

"Please." Her face colored with a quick blush. "Won't you come in?"

The boy, saying nothing as Tilman stepped into the hallway, took Tilman's hat and hung it on a well-polished hall tree. As Tilman would have expected, there wasn't a speck of dust anyplace he could see. She led him into a pleasant though sparsely decorated parlor and indicated a chair by the window. "Do sit down Mister Wagner. I'm Catherine Stone, and this is my son James." The boy watched from the parlor door, then stepped up and solemnly shook Tilman's offered hand. "James idolized Dan, and I'm afraid he's not gotten over losing him." She paused, "I'm sorry, you must think I'm terribly rude to speak so when we've only just met. First, would you like a cup of coffee?"

"Ma'am, thank you, but I don't wish to impose. Boy," Tilman turned to James, "would you lead that paloose of mine to a water trough and hitch him there? I believe he's mighty thirsty." Tilman had expected the widow lady to be old and wrinkled. Catherine Stone was neither. Young, probably early thirties, reddish-gold hair, blue eyes, and a spray of freckles across her nose, all in all a handsome young woman.

Looking eagerly at his mother, who nodded okay, the boy said "Yes, sir," and was out the door. In his haste, the door slammed as he jumped off the steps, welcoming an old friend in Dan's horse. "Hey, Needles, how you been, boy?" He and the horse ambled away from the house, the horse seeming to remember the small boy. Sounds of whinnies and laughter floated through the open window, both horse and boy apparently glad to see each other again.

"Thank you for that." Catherine paused, "James hasn't done a lot of laughing lately. It is good to hear he still can."

She turned to Tilman, a small but perceptible shift of her shoulders. Sadness? He didn't know. "Let me get that coffee. I could do with a cup myself. Believe me, it's no trouble and gives me an excuse to sit a minute." She smiled. "I've been doing battle with my favorite oval rug." She disappeared into the kitchen, leaving Tilman for the moment to look around. Most people seemed to believe that the more knickknacks and geegaws in a parlor the better, till a body could hardly move without knocking into something. Tilman was pleasantly surprised and comfortable. A worn Bible rested on a small table by her chair. Probably where the widow did her morning reading. "How can I help you?" Catherine brought the coffee and sat in a rocker, her hands calmly placed in her lap, her pose exuding a quiet serenity.

"I've come to find the man or men who killed my Dan, and wanted to call on you first to thank you for making sure he got a good burial, and to settle up his accounts. I'll move his things out of your way. I appreciate what you did for him." Tilman sipped the coffee. "Good coffee, ma'am. Pitch black, the way I like it. Must come from my Army days."

"Mister Wagner, his things are not in my way." Tilman knew that she told the truth and he would only insult her if he pushed the issue. "If Dan knew you were here he would want you to stay with James and me. You'll find the town is not a friendly place, so may I offer you Dan's room while you stay here in the valley? I've left his room just as he did." A tear welled up in her eyes. "You might want to look at it, and then refresh yourself and rest so we can talk." She showed Tilman Dan's room, the washhouse, and pointed out the clean towels, hot water and soap for a bath when he returned with his belongings.

"There are natural hot springs on the property," she said, "and some say they have medicinal powers, if you want to try them while you're here." She paused. "Last winter Dan would go out there and sit in them, even when there was snow on the ground!" She laughed. "He said I should order a bathing outfit from St. Louis so I could try it."

She left laughing while Tilman had a quick image of her in one of the newfangled swimming suits he had seen on ladies in the Sears catalogue pictures over at the general store. Shaking his head at such images, Tilman fleetingly wondered if Catherine and Dan had been more than friends. She was older than Dan, but then he had known several men to marry older women out in the West and, he had to admit, she was a woman who put thoughts into a man's head. Distracting. That was the word he'd use if asked.

He looked around Dan's room. Not much to show for a lifetime. A couple of shirts, worn but clean, hung on the clothes rack, and a pair of faded jeans was neatly folded in the drawer along with a couple of bright handkerchiefs and some rolled socks and underclothes. A few books were stacked by the twin bed and a picture of Sarah, faded and worn with time, looked up at Tilman from the dresser top. In the corner of the dresser, a stack of old letters worn and creased from rereading, were tied together with a piece of ribbon. Tilman didn't have to look at them to know that they were letters he'd written to Dan. He held them in his hand as regrets flooded his mind. He always meant to write more, always meant to visit more, always meant to do so many things, but the need to lash out after Sarah was killed was always so great. Tilman groaned inwardly, aware of his failure as a father. He replaced the letters, turned, and went to town to get the rest of his things.

Chapter Seven

The lady and her son had a big black kettle of water near boiling on the laundry stove in the washhouse by the time Tilman got back from town and had moved his gear into Dan's room. With a cake of lye soap Tilman scrubbed a week's worth of travel off his weary hide. The shave felt mighty fine, as did the clean clothes pulled from his war bag.

Early evening found Tilman perched on one of Catherine's three-legged stools at her small side table; hands around another steaming cup of coffee, as he looked around the tidy kitchen. There was a glass vase on the table, and in it were white marigolds. Tilman wondered if she was the one who left the same kind of flowers at Dan's grave.

"Mister Wagner," Catherine began, "I know there is much you wish to learn about what happened to Dan, and I will tell you all that I know. However, I feel I should tell you that I had my reasons for arranging Dan's burial and asking Mister Pegram—Butter—to wire you." She looked directly into his eyes, almost a challenge.

"Ma'am, I don't—"

"Please, call me Catherine. We are going to have to work together if justice is to be served, so let us not stand on formalities."

"Go on, I'd like to hear what you think." Willful, Tilman thought. She's been on her own long enough, she doesn't hesitate to speak her mind. Tilman began to see the Widow Stone in a new light. A woman of the West, full of dreams in her youth, and now a one-time ranch wife and mother who had become a widow operating a legitimate boardinghouse; the work was beginning to wear her down. But there was a sense of earnestness, a determination about her. Where did that come from? Had there been something between Dan and the widow?

"I've been a widow since James was five years old. I grieved, and I've made my peace with the Lord and moved on, taking care of James with what little his father left, making do with the ranch and by taking in boarders. When Dan came here last year, we soon became close friends." She sighed, a small smile on her lovely face. "We shared the same faith and the same dreams. He often helped out around the place, and with James. He was a fine gentleman." She turned to look out the window, and then looked back at Tilman. Catherine seemed to look into Tilman's soul, and it was as if she understood the darkness hidden there. "You really didn't know him, did you?"

Surprise and then confusion showed in Tilman's face. Close friends? She was a woman at least ten years older than his boy, Tilman thought, but she knew Dan better than he did. He started to deny her accusations, but paused. She was right. He didn't know his boy at all and now it was too late. He nodded agreement, and then busied himself by getting up and pouring another cup of coffee.

She stood and walked to a cupboard by the cook stove, removed a cloth-covered dough tray, placed it on a counter, and began pounding down the risen dough with a small fist. The room filled with the homey smell of yeasty batter.

"I didn't mean to pry," she continued. "I see by the look on your face that all this puzzles you. Dan and I met only last year. I know that I am older than Dan by several years, but our love of life became the basis for our close friendship. Oh, for a while there was talk in town about 'the widow's got her a young man.' Small-minded people talked." She smiled. "We were just friends."

She had a way of looking directly into Tilman's eyes that frankly made him a little awkward—even at his age!

She laughed softly, "Dan was probably looking for a mother, I think."

"I don't hardly see how that would be possible, ma'am, a woman as young and attractive as you," Tilman said. "I mean, Sarah had dark hair and eyes—you don't look at all like her." Talk about tongue-tied. Tilman decided to shut up before he made things worse.

Blush spread over her freckled cheekbones as she busied herself kneading that dough. The lady knew Tilman was studying her, and unless he was mistaken she felt flattered.

"I'll take that as a compliment, sir, and thank you."

"If you pound that dough again, Catherine, it'll be a month of Sundays before it ever rises!"

Replacing the cloth cover on the tray, she put it away to rise again. She washed her hands in a bucket by the sink and dried them on her apron before she came to sit down at the table near Tilman, her eyes avoiding his the whole time. She sipped her coffee and then raised her eyes and smiled.

"We spent many an evening reading books and poetry, and discussing our lives. We realized that we were kindred spirits, the best of friends. Our caring was different. We loved each other, but as brother and sister." Catherine's eyes twinkled. "Maybe, I should say older sister."

"No, ma'am. I sure wouldn't say it like that." Tilman paused—was he that bold to say such things to a lady he'd just met? But eager to talk to someone about his son he forged ahead. "I have to say I didn't know his likes and dis-likes as well as I should. I kept meaning to spend time with him, but my life got in the way." Tilman paused. Memories flooded his thoughts and soon he was spilling the whole story to this woman over a fresh cup of coffee and outstanding cinnamon rolls that had mysteriously appeared before him.

"After Dan's ma was killed by Comanches, I sent the boy to live in Fredericksburg." For some reason it seemed important to Tilman that she understand. "I reckon he was about fourteen years old, big enough to do man's work, so I got him hired on at the stage company hotel there for twenty a month and board."

This Widow Stone had a way of getting a man to talk. Tilman guessed he owed her that much.

"I rode a rough trail back then. The Yankee government in Texas wouldn't allow us to re-establish our Ranger Companies for ten years after the war. They set up a so-called police force, all carpetbaggers, and the scum of the Union Army. A sorrier set of men you never saw. They were only good for robbing honest citizens, and wouldn't turn a hand to go after outlaws on the frontier. I rode with some men who used to be rangers, for we taken it upon ourselves to try and keep some of the outlaw riffraff away from good folks. I saw Dan maybe once or twice a year. We weren't what you'd call close, but that don't change a thing. I aim to kill whoever it was killed him." Tilman was seldom such a talker but she'd helped and had a right to know.

"Dan said you became a hard man after his mother died, and—"

"Was murdered by Indians, you mean." She winced when Tilman interrupted. "There's a difference." He had accepted the murder, dealt with it, but it was never far from his mind. Scratch the thin surface Tilman covered his feelings with and all the hate and hurt was there, boiling up again. How could she know that? It's not her fault. She was a good woman and he had no right to be angry with her.

"Yes, that's so. I'm sorry." The calm look returned as she regained her composure, "Dan said you were different in those days. After the Indians came you became distant, a man obsessed by your wrath. I must tell you that James is my whole life. I intend to raise him the best I can."

Tilman heard her condemnation of his ways, but let it pass without comment. Again, her eyes bored into his. "Mister Wagner, we'd discussed our faith and I know Dan was a godly man. You've a right to know that James and Dan were very close. The boy looked up to Dan as if he were his older brother. James liked to go with Dan to the stage station, and then Dan would take James to the general store and buy him licorice candy. After Dan was killed, James began to have terrible nightmares. He told me that two men came to Dan at the station and were angry. James is too young to understand but he thought Dan was worried. Now the boy is scared the angry men will come to kill him too."

Tilman stood and refilled his coffee cup. He felt awkward. This wasn't what he came for. He wanted vengeance, not this. Where was this conversation going?

"Anyway, now you know all that I know. Dan was a good, kind, and forgiving man. He did not hate the Indians who killed his mother, he hated no man." She was almost pleading now, and her hand reached out to touch Tilman's arm. "It's not easy for me to ask, but Mister Wagner, for Dan's sake and the sake of his memory, stop the killing. In the Bible it says, 'Vengeance is mine. I will repay.'"

She paused. "Leave it with the Lord. He will take care of this!" Catherine's eyes reflected her fear for a man she'd only just met.

His anger boiled up, twisting his face as well as his soul. Recoiling, she withdrew her hand as if she was suddenly aware that the man across the table was the pale horseman, Death himself. He'd come a thousand miles to find a killer, and find him he would. Tilman drew a deep breath.

"Catherine, where does it say, 'An eye for an eye?' I sure like that one better."

Tilman stood, looking for his hat, angry with himself for his reaction to her pleading. Why did he care what she asked? He barely knew the woman. Yes, she and Dan had been friends, but that was then and this was now, and he had no time for pleasantries from goody-goody people who didn't understand what he fought. The devil himself was eating Tilman's insides out and he wanted desperately to make the hurt quit. And he knew only one way to do that. Revenge! Starting for the door, Tilman paused, and looked back at Catherine, sitting at the table, her hand tightly clasped on the cross around her throat.

"I can't change what I am."

"No, Mister Wagner, you can't change what happened. We can never go back to the lives we once lived. But there is always hope. With help, a person can change."

What could he say? That he didn't know what she was talking about? Thank you for the coffee? Surely she did not deserve the hard feelings he brought to her home. He took a deep breath and got himself under control.

"Ma'am, I know I didn't give Dan the time he needed after his ma was killed. I'll think about what you've asked. But that's all I can do. I'm much obliged for the coffee. Now, if you'll excuse me, there's things need tending."

Tilman went to the barn and saddled the paloose, and from his saddlebag pulled the belted Colt .45 and buckled it on. The boy James crept into the barn and stood silently by the stall gate. He was a small boy, and had seen too much already in his young life. Tilman could tell he wanted to talk.

"Mister Tilman, I don't have a daddy, and a bad man shot Mister Dan. Will you teach me to fight?" He opened the gate, standing between Tilman and his mission.

"I'll tell you what I'll do." Tilman walked over to him, squatted to his level. "I'll show you how I keep boys from beating *me* up."

"Go on," he said, trying hard not to grin. "You're so big nobody can beat you up!"

Tilman grew up the youngest of five brothers, the older four all rough and tumble fighters and well known around

Cabarrus County where they lived. So Tilman showed James some of his hard-learned ways of fist fighting among boys— North Carolina-country style. Tilman learned the real mean eye-gouging, ear-biting stuff much later out in Texas, and he hoped this child never had to learn those ways.

"Son, knowing how to fight is a good thing for a man, but knowing *when* to fight is even better. If I show you this, you have to promise you won't be just like those bullies I saw you with, picking on boys who can't defend themselves."

"Oh no, sir, I promise." Tilman left the paloose in his stall and went out on the other side of the barn, away from Catherine's curious eyes. He didn't need another run in right now with her if he could help it.

"Well, when somebody wants to beat you up, you get your fists up in front of your face." Tilman showed him with exaggerated movements. "Elbows together in front of your chest, bend over a bit so your elbows cover your stomach too."

Tilman helped James get his arms up to defend himself. "See, if they swing at you, they hit your arms, not your nose," and Tilman swung gentle punches, landing on the boy's arms. Ow!" Tilman complained in a whining voice, "that hurts my hands. I don't want to fight you."

James laughed. It sounded good to Tilman's tired ears. When had he last heard a youngster laughing for the sheer fun of it?

"You practice that. They'll soon get tired of hurting their hands on your bony old elbows, so when they get tired then you can punch them in the nose and send them home crying."

James liked that idea, and after hitting, laughing, falling, and repeating that sequence for a while, he ran from the barn calling, "Mom look what I can do!" All at once James turned, hesitated, and quickly ran back to where Tilman squatted, put his two skinny arms around Tilman's neck, gave him a big hug, and with a face so red Tilman could hardly tell it from his hair, the boy turned and ran to show his mom his new skills.

Tilman came to Colorado fixing to kill a man, and now he felt . . . what? Catherine was a decent woman, and he'd no right to be attracted to her. She didn't need a man like him in her life. What kind of man did this make him? He knew the answer to that. A dead one, for not paying attention to the evil in that valley.

Chapter Eight

W hen Tilman came back in the barn after carefully checking around the house to see if Catherine might have missed anything that Dan had left, he found the boy already hitching up their mare to a hack and about to lead it around front. "Ma needs to go get some things from town," he explained. "I bet she was pretty pleased with my fightin' skills." He laughed out loud, quite happy with himself. He didn't notice that Tilman was deep in thought, trying to deal with all that had occurred that day.

Climbing aboard the paloose, Tilman rode out and took the road back toward town, giving the paloose· his head. Catherine watched from the front porch. The boy smiled and waved, but the widow did neither. Tilman had not gone far when he looked back and saw her pull the rig onto the road behind him. That woman troubled him. She was too kind and gentle for this place and these times. Mister Morris had said the shooter rode north and east up the slope of what he called Free Gold Hill, so it was time Tilman went up there to look around. But first, he needed shells, and when he got to town he stopped to buy a couple of boxes of .44s for his Winchester, along with a small bag of coffee beans.

"Be right with you, sir, soon as we fill this order," said the clerk. A serious young man, he appeared to be something of a dandy with his hair slicked down and parted in the middle, fancy sleeve garters and a high-fronted apron. Tilman looked around at the merchandise while he waited. Through the window he watched as Catherine pulled her hack to a stop by the ever-crowded sidewalk out front, and got down to tie her horse at the hitching post. There was something about that woman that drew the eye, that was for sure. In this grimy town she was pure like a clean sip of water from one of the high mountain springs as the snow starts to melt.

A passing drunk lurched to an uncertain halt in front of Catherine, blocking her way. "Hello m'sweet darlin'!" His words slurred. "How 'bout a kiss?" he said as he grabbed her arms and pulled her face to his.

"Let me go. You're drunk!" she cried, struggling and turning her face away from the foul creature. "Help!" A few of the drunk's friends cheered him on, as though they were viewing a play of sorts.

"Wha'sa matter? Too good for ol' Shorty? Hey, le's go git a drink. I c'n pay, darlin'."

Tilman quickly left the store and shoved aside several men who'd stopped to watch the spectacle but were doing nothing to help Catherine. Tilman grabbed the drunk by his collar and his belt and lifted him to his toes, causing him to lose his balance and sputtering, "Wha', who's 'at?" as he let go of Catherine.

Tilman gave him a quick bum's rush along the walk to a water trough and threw the man in head first, holding him under until he figured the drunk had swallowed enough water. Tilman pulled up a half-drowned man spluttering and gasping for breath.

"Listen carefully. If I ever see you come near that woman again, or any decent woman in this town, I'll bust your skull!" Tilman lifted him out of the trough, roughly jerked the man to his feet, turned him, and shoved him hard out into the street to drive home the point. "Now git!"

By this time one of the town constables, unable to ignore the fracas any longer, got off his duff and came to investigate.

"You there, what's going on?" he called to Tilman.

The constable was short, fat, and his uniform was about a size too small. His hat fell off as he crossed the street. He picked up the hat, looked at Tilman, plainly hoping the big man wouldn't cause a scene. The constable wavered, suddenly wanted a drink, and seemed fearful of what trouble he might get himself into because of a drunk.

"Stand fast, you." Tilman put his finger in the constable's face, stopping him in his tracks and then turning him to face the drunk. "There's the one you want." Tilman saw that the sidearm the man wore was rusty. Some law he was—reminded Tilman of those carpetbagger police in Austin.

The constable was not a brave man, and he sized up the situation quickly, saw the easy way out Tilman offered him, and collared the staggering drunk—the same man Tilman had seen when Morris showed him around the freight station. "Oh, it's you again, Shorty. The boss warned you about messin' with decent women, an' he ain't gonna like what you done."

It seemed odd to Tilman that the constable hadn't said "the sheriff," but "the boss." Like Butter said, this town was sewed up.

"Catherine, I'll see you home . . ."

"Thank you, Tilman," she said. She'd regained her composure quickly. "That's not necessary. I'll be fine. I'm sure he won't bother me again. I need supplies and you've got business to see to." She turned, her blue checked skirt swirling, and went into the store, ending the conversation and making the point that she'd be all right.

She really puzzled Tilman. Stowing his purchases in his saddlebags, Tilman mounted up and passed on through town, forded the shallow river and climbed up to the rocks Morris had pointed out. No trace of the gunman remained. From where he was he could see up north of town, on the same side of the river, railroad work crews cutting a couple of tunnels, so he rode the newly graded roadbed toward the crews. The whole valley lay before Tilman in the warm mid-afternoon sun, clumps of cottonwood making brilliant yellow patches separating the light brown grassy open spaces, scarred here and there by wagon roads. Shadows were already masking the steep slopes of the western wall of the valley. From here the town didn't look so bad and the view of the mountains was almighty pleasing.

When Tilman rounded a curve approaching the first tunnel dig he found the work crew laboring to bore through the granite outcrop in a steep slope.

"Fire in the hole!" The powder man cupped his hands to his mouth and shouted his warning several times.

Men scattered for cover like prairie chickens spooked by a coyote. The muffled explosion blew a cloud of dirt and rock out of the tunnel mouth, and with much swearing and "Ho, mule! Haw!" teams got ready to muck out the shot. The powder man went in to check the face of the cut. Finding all charges fired, he sounded, "All clear!"

A tool dresser laid out cutting steel and called, "Come an' get it, boys," to the coming shift on the face of the cut. A small group of men clustered around the steps of an office shanty, probably taking their work direction from a section boss. As Tilman rode up the men turned and walked away. The gent Tilman figured to be the boss watched, his eyes giving away nothing. He was a well-set man about Tilman's age, shirtsleeves rolled up over muscled forearms.

"Howdy," Tilman said, "you in charge here?"

"Afternoon. If you're looking for work, I need a hunter."

"No sir. It's a fact I'm hunting, but not to make meat," Tilman explained. "About a month ago, a feller rode up here to the grade from the town down yonder. He'd have carried a Sharps .50."

"Taylor's my name"—he stuck out his hand—"are you the law?"

"Name's Wagner," Tilman said as they shook hands, "I'm looking for the man who killed my only son, down there, with that Sharps. All the signs said he rode this way."

"We don't see many visitors. About a week or so ago we saw several cowboys working the draws up here, pushing cattle down the mountain. Used to see prospectors, but not many lately."

Tilman figured that was about all he was going to get, and was about to drift, but the man was not finished.

"Well, I remember about the middle of last month when we were back down the grade a ways. A man on a paint horse come down the trail from up there"—he pointed with his chin to Free Gold Hill—"up from the south. By his dress I'd say he was no cowboy. Rode on past us without speaking. Fellow wore fancy silver spurs—big two-inch rowels. Don't see Mexican spurs in this part of the country. There was a long rifle in his saddle boot."

"Any idea which way he went?"

"He followed our survey markers to the north. Couldn't have gone far, for we've started these tunnel cuts only in the past week, so he'd have had to go back down to the river or cross the mountain."

"Much obliged for your help," Tilman said. The boss man nodded and as he turned to go into the shanty said, "Good luck."

Not much to go on, but what the man said was some help. The time was right. A fellow in that line of work wearing spurs like that doesn't care if he stands out or who notices. Maybe he figured nobody cared. He'd be wrong about that, Tilman thought, going to be dead wrong. If the shooter turned east to cross the mountain, he could have gone to the railroad spur at Como or Fairplay, but there was no trail across the mountain that Tilman could see from here. Somehow Tilman had the notion that he didn't seem a man who'd rough it any more than he had to, and these mountains were rugged. But, if a man dropped down to the river, he could either take the stage road north to Granite, or on to the mine works at California Gulch, an easy ride.

Tilman had a hunch he should go to Granite and look around. In his saddle gear he always carried a small bag of corn meal, some jerky, coffee, and a bait of corn for his mount. Tied to his saddle in the bedroll was Tilman's old Army gum poncho wrapped around a wool blanket. He had lived through some mighty cold winters, rain, sleet and snow in Virginia, with no more protection than that during the war for Southern independence.

Tilman backtracked a bit and took the easy trail down to the stage road where he turned north in the gathering dusk, letting the long-legged paloose fall into an easy pace. He'd gone about five or six miles when the road crossed the river on a newly built bridge. Just about dark, Tilman turned east to follow a creek cut into the mountain and found a good spot for a camp. Several large spruce trees stood on a flat, while up the creek was a thick clump of aspen, their leaves already gone, and white trunks speckled with black scars. Tilman quickly gathered some dry sticks and soon had a small fire going under one of the spruce trees. What little smoke the dry wood made would be scattered in the tree branches, and no more fire than he made could not be seen very far away. Tilman heated water in his tin cup, crumbled some jerky in it, and when it boiled he sifted some corn meal in to make "cush." When night fell the clear sky showed stars by the thousands, and a black mass of the western mountains outlined against the last faint glow of day. The North Star sparkled and flashed blue-white higher in the sky here than in Texas, but Tilman found it comforting, familiar.

After cleaning his cup, Tilman kicked dirt over the fire, and after watering the paloose once more in the darkness led the animal up to the aspen grove. Tilman unsaddled the horse and with a few clumps of dry grass gave him a quick rubdown, and then picketed him in a patch of grass not yet browned from the frost. He took the bedroll and crawled into the thicket. West Texas *bandidos* taught Tilman never to camp where he ate, and always move his camp to a new location after dark. Most folks meaning to harm a body would look for a cook fire, and try to ambush a man there. That had saved Tilman's hide a time or two. The horse would give plenty of warning if anybody or anything tried to get near, and whatever got past him would make plenty of racket getting through the trees to Tilman.

Quiet at last, with not even a breeze stirring, Tilman shivered in the chill of the evening. He crawled into his blanket and looked up through the bare trees at the stars. An image of Sarah came to mind. Many a night he'd spent on the trail like this. If she'd lived, where would he be? She was not a sinful woman, but died at the hands of those Comanches. And how was it that Dan could grow to be a fine man only to be shot down in cold blood? Sarah was a good woman. That Widow Stone was probably a good woman too. There was a peace about them both Tilman could never know. Now the Widow Stone had lost her husband and her friend Dan, too, but she still had that calm, accepting way about her. Tilman had many questions, but few answers. The widow's face came to mind, her eyes bored into his as he drifted off to a troubled sleep. Her smile tortured him.

Chapter Nine

This is young man's work, Tilman thought. It was just past first light when Tilman looked around in the dim, gray morning, listening to the sounds of the world awakening. He had his Winchester in his hands. Mexicans out in the Big Bend border country always like to hit a camp just after daylight, so old habits wouldn't let him sleep. It was cold! When he moved, Tilman's joints popped like twigs snapping. His left wrist ached where it was broken once, and the stiffened scar over an old wound sent nagging pains up his side. He carried to this day some Yankee bullet fragments inside that wound.

It had taken a while to get the cold morning stiffness out of his bones. The paloose watched, ears up, like he was wondering what Tilman was up to. The horse didn't see or hear any danger, nor did Tilman, so after making a little fire, Tilman used his rifle butt to grind some coffee beans in a cloth, and then boiled coffee, Army-style, in his tin cup.

The road to Granite followed along the eastern side of the Arkansas. To make better time he stayed with it along the floodplain by the river. The stage road was narrow and built up with rock walls on the downhill side where it cut into the mountain.

The canyon carved by the Arkansas was narrow here and the town of Granite filled what little floodplain there was. The town boasted of a hotel, a store, a brewery, six or eight saloons, two fancy houses, a warehouse and a whitewashed two-story wooden courthouse along a single long main street. From there it spread up the hillsides. Two stage stations faced each other across the main street—one for the new fast coach company. The buildings were mostly slab shanties, hard-backed tents, and more dugouts spread among the prospect holes. The river had become thick, muddy, and fast flowing, and a continuous loud roar boomed down the valley from the north. Curiosity got the best of Tilman, so he stayed on the stage road and passed through the edge of town. Between Granite and Balltown he discovered the sounds came from a different way of mining, using water—hydraulics they called it. Two men stood atop a hill on the eastern side of the river, so Tilman rode up for a better view to see what they were looking at. The men turned out to be mining engineers for the Hail Columbia Company, decent fellows, who took the time to show him their maps and explain what he was looking at. They told Tilman he was seeing the most modern and efficient way to get to the placer gold.

"You see, as gold washes down from those mountains, being heavier than rock, it falls to the bottom of a stream, and works its way down to bedrock. In the old days, say ten or twelve years ago," the older of the two said, "getting at this gold took a lot of men and great amounts of back-breaking pick and shovel labor to move the huge overburden of gravel so we could get down to the bedrock where the gold had settled."

"This is what we're looking for," the young one interjected, proudly pulling three glass vials from his pocket and handing them to Tilman. "You can see the gold can be fine as flour, or like grains of sand, or nuggets."

He got the impression the young man was glad to talk to

somebody who knew less about gold than he did. Tilman reckoned the older gent was a hard taskmaster for his young pupil. The noise was deafening, even worse than the Guadalupe River in full flood down in the Texas hill country, and all talking was done in shouts. To the west lay the Twin Lakes, a natural glacial formation. Water from the lake was brought down the slope to the edge of the plain in a long wooden flume snaking across the hills, even running across a trestle in some places. Steam pumps raised the water pressure to force water through iron pipes thirty inches in diameter to nozzles so the jet of water would cut away entire hills, washing the soil away, leaving behind huge piles of cobblestones. The soil-laden water then washed placer gold to lines of wooden sluice boxes, where baffles trapped the fine grains of gold while the rest of the runoff flowed into the river. Tilman understood now the reason for the flow of muddy water he'd seen below the town.

There was neither grass nor any trees near the river. All the trees had been cut and sawed to planks to build flumes, shanties, and shoring to hold the massive piles of gravel, cobbles and boulders left behind when the soil was washed away. It looked as barren as the worst desert ever seen.

It was past noon and Tilman figured he'd about worn out his welcome with the engineers, so he headed back to Granite for a meal and a drink and a look around. The Palace, an actual wooden building, posted a chalkboard menu offering hot elk stew and cold beer, and seemed as good a place as any to start. The stuffy room was crowded with rough-dressed miners; the smell of stale tobacco smoke mixed with the musky sweat of unwashed bodies, spilled beer and sawdust assaulted Tilman's senses as he pushed through the bat-wing doors. Nobody seemed to take notice as he stood up to the bar and ordered a rye.

Saloons are the best places to get caught up on news on the frontier, and with the right questions a man could learn all worth knowing about local goings-on. The bartender seemed talkative, and when he poured a second rye, Tilman asked about the lay of the land to the north. As he lifted his drink a small man, obviously in his cups and mad at the world, jostled Tilman's elbow. Shifting his weight, Tilman leaned away from the man and sighed, knowing what was coming next. Like a chick following a hen, trouble often seemed to walk behind a man, or in this case, alongside him. He was right.

"You'd best watch y'self," the drunk sneered as he looked up at Tilman and clumsily sat his drink on the bar.

Turning, the little man held on to the side of the bar with one hand, trying to thrust his face up even with Tilman's. "Push me around an' I'm liable to tear down y' meat house."

"Back off you little guttersnipe!" boomed a commanding voice from across the room, abruptly ending all conversation in the saloon. A dapper young gent rose from his poker game and strode to the bar. His clothes made him a standout in this place—a silver brocade vest over an immaculate white linen shirt and a black string tie, dark baggy pants, all the style for the time, tucked into immaculately polished high boots. Tilman recognized Bat Masterson, his trademark derby tilted at a rakish angle.

"You, my friend," Bat said as he poked two fingers into the little man's chest, "are about to commit suicide. You might as well know the man you're bracing. Meet Tilman Wagner, a gunny who'd as soon kill the likes of you as look at you. No man alive has ever made him back down. He rides the cap rock country down in Texas, and if you were sober or had any sense at all—neither of which you will ever be guilty of—a rummy like you wouldn't dare to stand at the same bar with a man like him."

The drunk, looking from Bat to Tilman, began to shake visibly, drool wetting his beard stubble. Tilman almost felt sorry for the man. There was no reason to fight him, nor did

Tilman want to fight anyone, except the person who killed his boy. Besides that Tilman didn't think he was half as bad as Bat made him sound.

"Bartender," Bat smiled, "call the undertaker. Boys," he called out to the room, "we're going to have some entertainment!"

Turning to the now thoroughly cowed drunk; Bat stepped back, saying, "Go ahead and brace him."

"But I ain't heeled, Mister Masterson, honest. I di'n't know who he was."

"Throw this miserable little guttersnipe out, Jake, and don't let him back in here where men are drinking," Bat roared at the bartender, "and send us a bottle!"

Taking a table at the back of the saloon, Tilman noticed Masterson sat with his back to the wall so he could see the only entrances to the building, the front doors and a side door at the end of the bar. One of the serving girls brought them a bottle and two glasses, her eyes seeking an invitation to join the party. Masterson dismissed her with a curt "Go," not even noticing the disappointment in the girl's eyes. Tilman guessed to many Bat was a hero of sorts. Tilman knew him as the restless, driven man he really was, just as Bat also knew him, he was afraid. Like knows like.

Pouring the first drink, Masterson's pale blue eyes revealed nothing when Tilman turned his glass bottom side up.

"Later, maybe."

Masterson nodded, and said in a low voice, "You're a long way from your home range, aren't you? What brings you this far from your stomping grounds?"

"Remember back in Dodge City first time we met?" Tilman reminded Masterson. "You were visiting your brother, it was back in '76, and you'd just been offered the job as deputy city marshal."

"That's right," Masterson said. "Wyatt Earp. He was assistant city marshal back then and made the job offer. I became a deputy marshal alongside my brother, Jim. I could handle a gun, y'see, but Jim didn't like to use one. Anyway, did you know those Ford County rascals voted me out of office this year? Too rough for their tastes, I reckon. I was heading for Tombstone when a railroad job came up down by Pueblo." He smiled. "I just turned twenty-four, and I want some excitement. Nothing's going on here, so I might drift pretty soon."

Tilman didn't remember Masterson as such a talker, and guessed the man must be lonesome for company. "Well, I didn't know you that night you collared a *vaquero* from a Texas outfit, that man who'd knifed a fancy house girl. You drew a crowd and didn't see his pard coming up behind you. I laid my gun butt behind the ear of the one fixin' to back-shoot you. Masterson, I figure I saved your bacon." Before Bat could speak, Tilman continued. "Wait, don't say anything yet. I remember after you introduced yourself you bought me a drink. But I saved your life, and you still owe me."

Masterson nodded agreement, and said, "Then what, or who, brings you here?"

"Personal reason. Somebody killed my son in Mahonville a while back." Tilman leaned across the table. "I aim to find whoever did it and kill him, so I need information. You were a good lawman. You always had a string of folks kept you informed of what was going on and I don't imagine you've changed as far as that goes." Tilman tried to read Bat's expression. "I figure you know most of what goes on around here."

Masterson's eyes constantly scanned the crowd in the room, his face giving away nothing. "Knowledge is power, Tilman. You've heard me say that before. No, I've not stopped learning all I can wherever I go." He sipped his drink. "It's kept me alive. Now, trust nobody in that town for even the law has been bought. The madams in the fancy houses take up a monthly collection and pay the policemen's salaries.

"There are two you need to know about, two men who

split all the action in that town. Ward, goes by the name 'Big Bill,' from no place in particular I know of. He supposedly came to town last year, throwing a lot of money around, and 'Smiley' Charbonneau, late of New Orleans. I hear if it won't stand the light of day they're in it somehow. Maybe they're not involved in killing your son, but they'll likely know who was. I hear Ward hires most of his dirty work so he'll seem respectable, but watch out for Smiley—he doesn't care and he's an artist with a knife." Bat paused to watch two men arguing loudly at the bar, and then continued. "Charbonneau backs all the houses in Mahonville's red light district, and takes a cut from all the gambling on the south side of Main Street. He works out of Mollie Green's St. Louis Parlor House. Ward has the north side, and hangs out at the Silver King Saloon in the evening."

Masterson tossed off a drink. "Now, Ward's set up a good front—he owns a dry goods store and part of a bank, and is known to be an easy touch for a grubstake. Claims he's a law-and-order man, regular churchgoer, a real friend of the 'down and out' and makes no secret that he is part of the Committee of Vigilance and Safety—a pack of night-riding murderers all. You cross them and they'll come some night and stretch your neck for you, if you haven't already turned up dead along the road. Ward appears to have his hands in most everything else that'll make him a profit. People say he's got something big in the works. I don't yet know what, but something going with some pretty rich ores. And that's mighty interesting since he's not a miner."

Pistol shots suddenly erupted at the bar. Both men jumped to their feet, chairs tumbling backwards, their hands holding half-drawn six-shooters in time to see one of the argumentative drunks already down and the other standing there calmly shooting at him. Men were scattering to get out of the way when the bartender, Jake, clearly a man not to be trifled with, leveled a cut-down shotgun across the bar and let go both barrels with a mind-numbing roar in the close room.

The drunk slammed several steps back where he crumpled to the floor, dead, his gun hand covering his forever-still chest as if the undertaker had already been on the scene. The acrid smell of gun smoke spread through the room.

"Great God A'mighty," somebody said in awe.

The two drunks had gone from an argument to a gunfight in the blink of an eye. "Somebody go get the sheriff," the bartender said, as he coolly opened the breach of the shotgun, dropped the smoking spent shells to the floor and replaced them with fresh loads.

Tilman looked back at Bat and noticed the color had drained from his face, his breathing shallow and fast. He's losing his nerve, Tilman thought as they sat back down. This place had Tilman on edge too. Nobody sat down near them.

Conversation began again; men stepped around the bodies as if sudden, senseless violence and death were a common occurrence. Who were those men who had just died? Did they have families here, or back in the States? Life seemed to have little value in this valley; this place was as bad as any Tilman had seen in his years on the Texas frontier.

"Bat, do you ever get tired of this? Always looking for somebody out to get you? Do you ever think it's time to move on and settle down somewhere, get respectable so you can die in bed of old age?"

Masterson smiled grimly. "I came out here to ramrod a pack of gunslingers for one of the railroads in what the papers called the Royal Gorge War. It didn't amount to much of a war, so I'm cuttin' loose. Tombstone has been on my mind, and over there I'll be just an ordinary citizen. Be nice to not always be looking over my shoulder." When he poured himself another drink the bottle chattered on the shot glass. "You, Wagner, had enough?"

Tilman turned his glass over and filled it. "Not until I find who killed my son. Then, who can say? This is the only life I know." He tossed off the raw whiskey, felt it burn in his throat, and stood up. "I came in here to get a bite of grub.

Let's find a quieter place so I can eat." Suddenly Tilman just wanted out. Out of the slime and depravity that many of these people had come to. Unbidden, a picture of Catherine working in her kitchen with dough up to her elbows came to Tilman. He paused, his thoughts on her.

"You coming, Tilman?" Bat stood at the side door, a quizzical expression on his face.

Pushing his hat on, Tilman followed Bat outside.

"Sorry, must be getting old or something. Forgot where I was for a moment." The door slammed behind him leaving the sounds of despair within the thin walls of that thrown-together saloon.

For more than a week after his return from Granite, Tilman rode through the town and nearby countryside, and sat for hours in saloons to listen, watch, and ask discreet questions. Tilman knew from experience that the one way to find out what was going on was to invade the places where the enemies were. He nursed weak drinks, played the part and always listened. Many loose ends of information came his way, but so far none pointed definitely to any one man who would pay for Dan's death.

Skinny Morris, kind and apologetic, seemed to be haunted by a question he'd repeated several times over coffee— wasn't there anything he could have done the day Dan was shot that might have helped? He wanted to help Tilman in order to make up for what he thought were his own failings that day. He had given Tilman a small rock, ordinary and grayish looking with flecks of colors in it. He suggested Tilman get it assayed, and told him the name of a trusted assayer who could keep a confidence. He said the rock came from one of the bags Shorty Bain unloaded the day Morris told Tilman how Dan had died. Tilman thanked him, said he'd get it done. What had Morris risked to get that rock? What did he want Tilman to know about it? Why was it important to him that Tilman know Shorty Bain was involved? How was any of this related to Dan's murder? The answers were elusive, and bred only frustration.

In the back of his mind Tilman worked and worried at what he knew, confident that as in the past the pieces would simply fall into place and he'd know what to do. What did he know about Ward and Charbonneau? Which could be safely ignored, freeing Tilman to concentrate on the one more likely to have wanted Dan killed? Charbonneau seemed the lesser problem, for the way he operated just didn't seem to meet the description of what Tilman thought he was looking for. Charbonneau's trade was slick, but somehow the devil he dealt with seemed to have nothing to do with anything Tilman's boy might have been mixed up with.

Ward was out of town according to the rumors and not expected back for a while so Tilman didn't know much about what he looked like, just that he seemed to have his hand in everything that was going on in Mahonville, and around the county as well. Smiley's evil stemmed from his penchant for fallen women and involvement with the parlor houses. Ward's came from . . . well, from what?

Catherine watched from her window as Bill drove his bright, ebony-polished carriage into her yard. He was the answer to a widow's prayer in that he offered security and standing in Mahonville. He would pay off the ranch and James would be guaranteed a place to call his own when he grew up. So why did she feel a sense of unease she couldn't identify? Bill was a leader of the community, a man said to be wealthy, and a man who would be a leader of the state before he was finished. She knew James didn't care much for him. That was evident by the fact that he was nowhere in sight. She wasn't sure where this dislike came from, and while nothing was ever said she knew it existed.

Bill hitched his horse to the post. Like his owner, this ani-mal was sleek, well fed, and high-strung. The man fascinated her. "You ninny," Catherine admonished herself. "What did you have for lunch? Your imagination is running wild again." Catherine's mother used to say that to her when she would say something out of the ordinary when she was growing up. Funny, she reflected, how old memories came floating into your mind at the strangest times.

"Hello the house! Catherine? Are you in there?" Bill's voice came from the front door, and Catherine suppressed a small feeling of guilt and let the lacey curtains fall back in place, and smoothed the front of her second-best skirt, a muted red plaid that reminded her of the fall. She went to let him in.

"Come on in, Bill. Brr. It's getting cold outside." Taking Bill's expensive black bowler, Catherine offered him her cheek for a small kiss, and then led him into the parlor. She placed the hat on the hall tree, wryly thinking, yes, he and his horse are both sleek and well taken care of, that's for sure. "Would you like some fresh cookies, Bill? I just made them this morning."

"No, thanks, Catherine, honey," he said patting his thickening middle, quickly looking around the bright, shining parlor. "Can't be indulging too often in things of excess now, can we?" He sat in the loveseat, looking at her as though he expected her to join him. Catherine moved to her old, well-worn rocker instead and adjusted the oil lamp. From his immaculately tailored coat he produced a small, gaily wrapped package and placed it in Catherine's lap.

With a small cry of delight, she opened it, finding a tiny bottle of exquisite perfume, and murmured her thanks. "Bill, you mustn't. But it's lovely," she said as she touched the bottle's lip to the inside of a wrist. "I'll only wear it when you visit."

Smoothly, Bill complimented her on how charming she looked, and how thrilled he became whenever he thought about calling on her. Bill Ward had a way with words that would appeal to any woman. No one had ever talked to her quite that way, nor had anyone been so attentive with bouquets of flowers, French chocolates, and small, affectionate notes delivered when he was out of town. She always enjoyed hearing stories about his adventures in Denver and St. Louis, romantic-sounding places she'd never been to. Tonight's adventure dealt with a recent trip he had just returned from in Colorado Springs, where he had stayed at the Broadshire, a beautiful new hotel that housed the best of all worlds. "Some day you and I will make a trip there, Catherine, honey. You won't believe the size of the suites. Why"—he swept the room with a large hand—"the room I stayed in was the size of this parlor and the kitchen put together." Bill keenly followed her response to his suggestion. Catherine sat still, not sure what to make of his statement, fraught with innuendo.

The magic was soon broken, as Bill seemed to realize that James was not in the house. "Where is that young son of yours? Out getting in trouble?"

Why did he always say things like that about James? Catherine thought he must not ever have been around children.

"He is studying at Bob Lytle's house. The boys have an arithmetic test tomorrow and so they are working overtime." No need to mention that James practically ran out the door when he heard that Mr. Ward was coming. Was she missing something? The one thing she knew was that there was no love lost between the two of them. Before she could continue that thought, Bill moved over on the end of the loveseat closer to her rocker.

"So that means the two of us are alone here for the evening?" He adjusted the turquoise stone-mounted clip on his bolo and smoothed the black leather vest he always wore. The smile that played on the corners of his lips never quite seemed to reach his eyes. Or was it just the lamplight?

"No, Bill, it isn't just the two of us." Catherine patiently picked up a small quilt on which she was working a delicate wedding band pattern in varying shades of blues. Her lively eyes sparkled, "Mister Wagner is in the back in his room. He brought in some type of mining reports that he got from the assay office and he was deeply involved in reading them. Hardly ate anything for dinner, he was in such a hurry to get back to those papers. Also Pastor Fry is staying here, although he is still out on a call."

"What kind of assay papers?" Bill wasn't interested in Pastor Fry.

"I don't know, Bill, just some papers. You know he's looking into his son's death and so maybe that has something to do with it. Maybe he's taken up prospecting. I don't really have any idea." Catherine laid her quilting on the table. "Are you sure you don't want something to drink? You look unsettled." She started to get up and go to the kitchen.

Before Bill could speak, the back door slammed and James came bounding in. All at once the room seemed to shrink in size as his youthful energy filled the parlor. "Hi, Mom. Forgot a book." He nodded to Bill. "Evening, Mister Ward. Excuse me." He flew back out the room, Catherine and Bill could hear books falling on the floor and then he was out the door again, slamming the screen, his mouth apparently full of cookies as he hollered, "Be home in a little while, Mom."

Bill stood, pulling a gold watch from his vest pocket as he checked the time. "Guess I better head on out. I just remembered some business I need to take care of this evening as well, Catherine."

Following him to the door, Catherine noticed he kept looking down the hall to Tilman's room. Strange, she mused, how concerned he was about Mr. Wagner's whereabouts and goings on. "Do you really have to leave so soon, Bill?"

"Better get on the road. It is a way back into town and the bears have been down some lately trying to get a last-minute meal before they take that long winter's nap." He looked at Catherine. "I am surprised you let James out this late."

"Bob's house is only the other side of our fence. You know that, Bill. Besides, any bear that went after James would just toss him back. He is too skinny for his own good." Catherine and Bill both laughed at the picture of James and a bear confronting each other.

Catherine watched as Bill took his leave. He must be conscious of the appearance he made—but it was true; they seemed to be a well-groomed pair, he and his mighty horse. Catherine picked up her quilt to put it away, her eye catching the reflection of a picture frame in which Henry, her late husband, stood grimly posed for the Daguerre process portrait made back in Pennsylvania. Tonight it seemed as if he watched her, wanted to ask her a question. Did he wonder what she was getting herself into? He couldn't realize how hard it was to be alone in the West with a young child who needed an education and shelter. Bill Ward offered security to her. The questions of doubt that perplexed her from time to time were surely just normal. They had to be. Hearing James at the back porch, Catherine closed the door on her uncertainties and went to join her son.

Chapter Ten

Sleep eluded Tilman as usual and so he found his way to a comfortable rocking chair on the spacious front porch of the boarding house. Moonless night gave way to day as the sun edged up over the mountain rim on the eastern side of the valley to paint everything with warm golden light. When the first rays of the morning washed over him he marveled at how quickly its warmth pushed away the night's chill to bring a sense of renewed hope, even to him.

Someone stirred inside the house. The screen door hinges creaked behind him. That someone stepped onto the porch and eased the screen door closed so the spring didn't slam it shut.

"Morning, Mister Wagner. Mind some company?"

"Morning, Paul." Putting those troubling thoughts of Dan out of mind, Tilman looked at the preacher. Bare-headed, and wearing patched white socks with gray toes, Paul Fry wore dark woolen trousers held up by galluses and an open collared white shirt—first time Tilman'd seen him without his coat and string tie. "Sure, pull up a chair. I'd like to sit and talk a spell. Mornings are good for that. My Sarah and I used to take coffee in the morning while the boy was still asleep and before the work was calling . . ." Tilman faded off, lost in distant time.

When Paul finally settled, the men sat and rocked silently for several long minutes. Tilman had the feeling the man was studying him.

"If someone would get that door," Catherine's voice floated on the morning air from inside, "I've some fresh coffee for you early risers."

Both men rose, Tilman removed his hat and Paul got the door. A faint scent of lavender floated through the air as Catherine, moving with a grace one did not expect to find in such rough country, placed a brightly polished silver serving tray and a coffeepot with a sugar bowl, creamer, and some delicate china cups and saucers on a wicker table. Joining them, she said with a smile, "Today is going to be busy, with the revival and picnic and everybody within twenty miles coming for the day. I seldom get a chance to use my silver and good china here, so you gentlemen may consider yourselves fortunate guests indeed."

"Fortunate, yes," Paul replied grinning broadly, "but not for the material things, such as the fine silver. It's a glorious moment for us to share the beauty of this morning and the company of such a lovely lady, another fine creation." Pastor Fry was rewarded with a beautiful smile.

Tilman found himself foolishly wishing that he had said that. Catherine busied herself pouring the coffee. A genteel woman of the old-time South couldn't have done a more elegant job.

"Please gentlemen, do sit down."

The coffee was strong and hot. They watched the sunrise. Tilman had the feeling he was about to be ambushed.

"Tilman, lately when you return from the town, you've been spending more and more of your time out here, alone." Making a show of stirring her coffee, Catherine asked, "Do you want to talk about it?"

"Sometimes it helps to share a burden," Paul said quickly, adding, "You'll not offend me, nor will you surprise me, most likely. Before I heard the call to become a man of the cloth, I walked many different paths. Maybe I can even help in some way."

"What have you, a preacher, ever done that you'd understand what I must do?" Tilman snapped, more sharply than he'd intended.

Catherine stood, saying "Oh, my. Do I smell something burning? I've some cinnamon rolls in the oven. I'd better go see to them." As she turned to go inside, a look passed between her and Paul. Tilman was right. He'd been ambushed.

"Mister Wagner, when I was a young man I rode with Sheridan's cavalry up the Shenandoah Valley in 1864, when we burned and pillaged at will, and left nothing for those poor souls to make it through the winter on. Sheridan hand-picked us, wanted us tougher than Reb cavalry, and we were—most of us seventeen or eighteen years old, no more than a hundred and forty-five pounds, born for the saddle and handy with a gun. I'll never forget one old woman. The boys killed her goose and she just cried, and said 'You 'uns is nothin' but dirty Yankees after all.'" He studied Tilman's face as he spoke. "I was a cruel man in a harsh time. Men we thought to be guerrillas, we mostly just hanged them on the spot." He turned to look out across the valley, and Tilman could tell his mind was back in those old times. "Sometimes we'd give them a horse and a twenty-five yard start, but we were all crack shots with a pistol and a carbine, and we made sport of it."

He turned back. "Sport of killing. After the war, I came west because I couldn't go back to working in a factory in Providence. I needed excitement. Well sir, I rode a rough trail and found more than I bargained for."

Tilman watched as Paul opened his shirt front, pulled aside his undergarment to reveal five bullet scars on his upper chest, the healed flesh smooth, raised, and still discolored a pale purple. From their placement, Tilman would have pronounced any one of them mortal. Whoever patched him up sure knew a lot about treating gunshot wounds.

"I was drinking in a parlor house one night, got into an

argument over one of the 'ladies' with my pard. He did this. I believe I died for I saw the bright light, even saw myself lying there on the carpet, as if I were standing back looking over the shoulders of the folks working over me." He paused. "But a voice told me the time was not right and I should go back for I had the Lord's work to do."

"Paul, you don't expect me to believe that, do you?"

"I'm just telling you what I used to be." He smiled.

"What does this have to do with me?" Didn't Sarah tell Tilman about a Paul in the Bible? Old Preacher Sharp back home would never have stood for Tilman to call him by name, nor would Tilman have dared.

"Mister Wagner, no matter who we are and what foul deeds we've done, forgiveness and salvation are to be had if we only ask. You're here seeking vengeance against the man who killed your son. Leave that vengeance. The Lord knows why it happened, and He's the only one can understand it."

"When we ask for forgiveness for what we've done to others, we must also be ready to forgive what others have done to us," Catherine said, stepping back out onto the porch.

Tilman growled, "For such a lovely creation, you can sure worry something to death, Catherine!" He stood up, and moved to the edge of the porch.

"Now look here," Tilman snapped, his temper rising, "I came to find and kill a killer. If you really want to help me, then hear this. I'm at a dead end. No matter how many people I talk to it's always the same. Nobody in town knows anything. It's as if Dan never existed." Cold anger had him and he couldn't stop.

"Butter told me that two men have this town sewn up tight. Bat Masterson told me the same thing. I keep coming back to these fellows Ward and Charbonneau, just because I can't think of anyone *else* might have done it. I'm ready to call them out and send them both to the fires of hell just because they seem to be the worst of the lot."

Catherine walked to the end of the porch and sat in the

swing. "Charbonneau is indeed a person no one will ever blame for a decent act," she said, "but I disagree with what you and that Masterson person says about Mister Ward." Looking at the pastor for reassurance, she continued. "He never misses church, does he, Pastor?" Warming to her subject, she went on. "He set up a fund at the Valley Bank for the aid of widows and orphans in our community. People say that he is always ready to stake a prospector who is down on his luck. Why, he even asked if he could come calling on me, and only a gentleman would ask such a thing of a widow."

As if she realized she'd gone too far, she blushed, picked up a book from the wicker table by the swing and started to read.

"It's true," Paul said, although Tilman detected a slight hesitation before he answered. "Mister Ward attends all my services when I'm in town, and I've come to depend on his rather generous donations for our mission to this valley."

Whatever Paul said next Tilman didn't hear, for when he looked at Catherine he was stunned to see her wipe away a tear. When she looked up she caught Tilman staring at her. She stood and left the swing, bringing Tilman the book in her hand.

"This was Sarah's," she said. "I took it from Dan's room after he was killed so I could enter his death on the family page, but, oh, I found so much suffering revealed there. It grieved me to read it." She sighed. "I much preferred the pages of births and baptisms. I know it's foolish, but I . . . oh, never mind." She thrust the book into Tilman's hand and went back to her swing, her foot tapping nervously on the wooden porch.

Tilman accepted the Bible, but the lump in his throat kept him from speaking. He guessed she knew that because she said nothing more. Tilman wanted to know but was afraid to ask. Could Sarah's and Dan's death be on *his* shoulders because of all he had had to do in the war?

"What kind of truth stops me every time I try to do what I *know* needs to be done? Is it one that lets an outlaw win?

That kind of truth is not one for me. What am I supposed to do?" Tilman was not ready to hear their answers for he knew what he had to do. He was consumed with hate and a desire for vengeance. "I need to think about this." Tilman mumbled thanks and excuses and knew that if he looked he'd see pity on their faces. He didn't want or need that, so he couldn't get away fast enough. Tilman made his way to the back of the house by the clear-running stream. It was not enough that he was troubled by his inability to find Dan's killer, but now he had all these questions to think about and no easy answers either.

Tilman had not been sitting long when neighbors and folks from town and the neighboring farms and ranches began to arrive. Some rode in light buckboards, some jolted up the road in old springless farm wagons with colorful handmade quilts piled in the back as cushions for the ladies and children. Others came on horses, but all for the church service in Pastor Fry's green-and-white-striped tent. Many brought picnic baskets.

Apparently this revival and picnic was a big event in Mahonville. The tent was set up on Catherine's property on the far side of her house under a large stand of majestic cottonwood trees. A sense of longing for a family and no worries as he enjoyed long ago swept over Tilman.

As happens in most established but isolated communities where there was not much change in the population, young folks tended to marry the neighbor's son or daughter. Because of that, many of the families were related for they had been in this small valley for years. Church revival meetings and reunion dinners were a way for members who lived on opposite ends of the valley to get together socially to see how children had grown, talk about crops and animals, make music and tell stories.

Tilman watched Catherine greet one of the men who arrived on a fine, big dun horse. She had changed into a dress that seemed to be the color of the stream he sat by. Its blue-green texture shimmered and rustled as she walked. Sarah had a dress like that when they lived in North Carolina. Hers had been deep red though. It's funny how one remembers such things. When the man stepped down, Catherine stood close and put her hand on his arm as they talked. Tilman felt a stir deep inside—why? Why was she touching him like that? The intimacy of that gesture took him by surprise; it was the way a wife touches her husband. Jealousy? Certainly not! But there was no denying it: He envied the man that touch. Tilman wanted her to touch his arm that way. Both turned to look in his direction.

Then Catherine, hands on her hips, seemed to be having words with James, who had come when his mother motioned to him and now stood behind her, head down as he studied the ground. James took the reins from the man and led the horse off to a hitching rail, while Catherine and the gent came towards Tilman.

"Mister Tilman Wagner, of Texas," Catherine said, "May I present Mister Bill Ward." She was being very formal, and also a bit nervous. The well-dressed, clean-shaven man standing before Tilman with outstretched hand was nearly as tall as he was, and probably some heavier due to the thickening around his middle. The man's thin smile went only as far as his narrow lips, never coming close to the steely blue eyes that assessed Tilman with great care. Shaking hands, Tilman found Bill Ward to have the soft hands of a man used to easy living, but a surprisingly strong grip. He'd done hard work somewhere, if not now then in the past.

"Howdy," Tilman said.

"Mister Wagner," he said with a cautious nod, "I've heard about you. My condolences about your son."

"Thank you." *What's this?* Tilman wondered who had been talking about him with this jasper.

"Excuse me, but I have things to attend to," Catherine said, "I'll leave you two to get acquainted."

The men paused, both watching Catherine as she gracefully departed. Tilman was right. Her dress rustled like the wind in the aspen trees.

"I knew it," Tilman said to no one in particular.

"Will you be staying long in Mahonville, Mister Wagner?" Ward's abrupt question brought Tilman back to the present in a flash.

"Long's I need." He studied the man. "Why?"

"Well, what I mean is, will you be staying on at Catherine's place?"

"I don't see that's any concern of yours."

"But it is. You see, she and I have been keeping company, and I don't like your staying there. People in town will talk and such talk is damaging to a woman's reputation." He paused as if considering whether to go on or not. "I told your son the same, and he understood his mistake."

"Mister Ward, let's get something straight right now. Catherine runs a business, and I'm a paying customer. Nothing she or I have done calls for any talk in that town. Anybody who has any questions or anything to say can take it up with me. What passes between you and her is your affair, none of mine. I don't know you from Adam's off ox, so don't you ever try to tell me what to do unless you're ready to part company with some of those pretty teeth."

"You got nerve!" Ward said and swore a vicious oath. "Can you back that kind of talk with your fists or do you need a gun in your hand?"

Tilman took a half step to Bill's left and back a bit— Tilman had the reach on Ward with his long arms, so he shifted his weight to the balls of his feet, fists clinched, ready to swing. He'd put Ward in an awkward spot to throw a right if it came to that. What was it about this man? He was trapped and could only react to Tilman's initiative. Ward knew Tilman could land the crucial first hard blows before he could be ready, and he probably also knew that in most fights, whoever lands the first punch usually wins the fight.

Hold! This is not the time or place, Tilman thought.

"Get out of Catherine's house, and get out of this town, Wagner," Ward spat, his eyes turning mean, all pretense of those good manners he put on for Catherine gone. "We deal harshly with your kind around here."

"Like with Dan?" Tilman tensed, wishing he had his gun. "Did you deal with Dan, Ward?" He wanted to throw that right straight to the man's chin. "Why wait? Can you back up those threats or do you need help?" Tilman challenged as he moved in close to grab Ward's shirt front and pull him close. "No man tells me when to stay and when to go. Now's as good a time as any. Your pick, friend—guns, knives, or fists, what do you like?"

Disgusted, Tilman backed off. What was he doing? Clearing his head, he took a deep gulp of fresh air, and realized he would not start a fight here, so he released the hold on Ward's shirt with a shove that sent Ward staggering off balance. "Get out of my sight."

Masterson had told him Ward hired his dirty work. Masterson was right. Ward lacked the courage to meet a real man face to face.

Tilman watched as Ward angrily turned away and strode to his horse, mounted, threw Tilman a hard look, and spurred to a gallop back down the hill toward the town. *I must have said something close enough to the truth to put him off,* Tilman thought. *Doesn't look like he's going to stay for church.* Catherine stood by the entrance to the tent, looking from Ward back to where Tilman stood, then turned and ducked into the tent. Tilman couldn't help but wonder how much she had seen.

So that was the Ward fellow Bat Masterson had talked about. Tilman had an urge to go wash his hands. Ward had made no bones about laying out a claim on Catherine. What else? He sure didn't seem to want Tilman to stick around. Was Tilman in the way of Ward's plans? Just what were his plans? The picture of Catherine and Ward didn't sit well at all. There was something shady about Ward, and Tilman couldn't see him as a father for James or a husband for Catherine, nor the good friend folks made him out to be. Something wasn't right and Tilman meant to find out what it was.

Turning around Tilman moved further down the creek bed and sat on a gnarled old stump. Wagons stopped, people unloaded their food for the luncheon after the revival, and children laughed and ran around, eager to see each other. Sunday revival or service was all the socializing some of the women and children in the West had. Farms and ranches were few and far between and unless the husband worked in town, most lived out and around Mahonville. Tilman didn't need to see what was happening to know what was going on. The memory was all too bittersweet.

A wide range of voices began the opening hymn, "Amazing Grace," with a fiddle and a guitar playing along. Pastor Fry, since he didn't have enough hymnals to go around, would speak a line and the congregation would then sing it. Back in North Carolina they called that "linin' it." Been many a year since Tilman'd heard that done.

Tilman grabbed up the Bible ready to sling it into the creek but a piece of paper fell from it. Picking it up he saw it was written in Sarah's hand. It was a letter she never got to send. A picture of Sarah writing by the fading lantern's light came to him.

My Dear Tilman,

I take pen in hand in the hope that this letter finds you in good health as you drive our cattle to New Mexico Territory. I wish you a safe and speedy return to our Texas home, for even though you have not yet left us I know I shall feel your absence deeply. I want you to know though how much I enjoy and cherish every minute we have together, as I have always done from the time we were children growing up in North Carolina till the time we find now with our son Dan. He tries so much to be like you. Our life has had its ups and downs but that is what life is about and I want you to know that I would never try to change one little thing. You are a good man and I am proud to be your wife.

Love,
Sarah

He'd always believed there are no coincidences because people make things happen. Sarah was reaching to him now, still trying. Why now? Why here?

Drawn, even against his better judgment, Tilman found himself at the back of the revival tent. The sun, high in the sky, provided needed warmth, as the day itself was cool and clear. The tent was filled with people from all over the valley. Tilman saw several of the town's leading drunks on one row, maybe looking for a little absolution. He smiled and slipped into an open seat on the back row.

Warmth filled this open-air tent, warmth from all the happy faces around him. Maybe the sun wasn't so needed after all. People turned to welcome Tilman, children wiggled on the hard planks that had been laid over stumps and rocks, and an elderly man snoozed away while his wife pinched him every few moments so he wouldn't fall off the board.

"Welcome, welcome, welcome, my friends," Pastor Fry started, pausing as his eyes swept the audience and saw Tilman, then smiled and continued. "I want to know if you love your brothers and sisters? Do you now?"

Voices were raised from all corners of the tent.

"Halleluia!"

"That's right, Preacher!"

"Amen!"

It had been years since Tilman went near a church, but Pastor Fry's tent meeting gave him an unaccustomed sense of peace. Tilman sat up straight and listened intently as Pastor Fry began to speak.

"Friends, loving your family is easy. Today, I'm going to talk to you about loving your enemies!

"Friends, the good book says we have to love each other as ourselves. That means we have to love ourselves first and then the other will come."

"My friend, if God can forgive you, why can't you forgive your enemies and each other?"

How could Tilman be forgiven for his past? He had spent many years doing things that were best not talked about. Lost in thought, Tilman didn't even hear the closing hymn or remember walking back out into the fresh air. He put his hat on and started to head back to the house.

"Mister Tilman, aren't you going to eat? My mom made one of her famous apple pies." James stood quietly beside Tilman.

Where had James come from? Tilman hesitated, and then said, "All right, boy. Show me the way."

Chapter Eleven

In the shade of tall cottonwoods by the stream, the women had placed planks on sawhorses, spread tablecloths of all sizes and colors over them, and the whole thing was sagging under the weight of custard, pecan, apple, and peach pies. Three-layer chocolate and spice cakes competed with German chocolate muffins, while large crocks of iced tea and buttermilk, fried chicken, venison, beef, biscuits, potatoes and green beans, pintos, and even fresh tomatoes completed the appealing fare. It was enough to make a man's mouth water. And there at the head of the line was a familiar face!

"Butter, what are you doing here?"

"My ma raised me to be a God fearin' man, an' I never miss a meetin' less I have to. Besides, looky here at this table." Butter laughed. "Now, I'm batchin' it, an' I reckon Skinny Morris is a fair cook for durin' the week, but if you think I'm about to miss such eatin' as this you either taken one lick on the head too many else you boys from Texas been a-eatin' loco weed!"

Pastor Fry said grace, and Butter, James and Tilman loaded up—it was "Here Mister Wagner, have some of this corn," and "My, James, are you sure you can eat all that?"

And "Mister Pegram, you better try some of that cornbread." Those ladies ushered the men through the line until they couldn't possibly put anything else on their plates. They found a shady spot, sat, and went to work.

Afterward, Butter pulled out his pocketknife, cut a sprig off a nearby scrub oak, deftly trimmed some toothpicks, and then passed them to James and Tilman.

"James, you been practicin' what I showed you?" Butter asked.

"Yes sir." James's red hair seemed to be made of flames as the afternoon sun reflected through the cottonwood branches. His happiness was so apparent at being with "the men" that it made Tilman stop to wonder that he had never taken the time to spend with Dan like this, merely sitting and jawing about learning to handle a team. The little things were what stood out.

"Young James here wants to learn how to drive a stage." Butter stood up and brushed the remnants of a piece of chocolate cake off his shirt. "C'mon, let's go in the barn."

Inside, Butter had set up an old buggy seat, and from the wall had strung some old reins, enough for three spans of horses. James climbed into his seat and gathered up the reins, carefully arranging them in his hands for Butter's inspection and approval.

"Mister Tilman, look." He showed how it was supposed to be done. "Hold the leaders' reins between the index and middle fingers of each hand." He looked to Butter for assurance that he used the right words, and at Butter's silent nod he continued. "The reins for the swings go here between the middle and third fingers, and between the third and little fingers you hold the reins for the wheelers." Having gotten all that right in the telling and the doing, his face broke into a huge grin. He held his hands in his lap, the way Tilman'd seen Butter hold his when he drove a stage. "This is how a top driver does it," James said proudly.

Butter patted the boy on the shoulder. "Well done, James."

They relaxed, full from their meals, and for a while not taken up with the affairs of the world. Reality reared its ugly head when James turned to Tilman and seemed to have something on his mind. He had started to speak several times, but never voiced whatever he was working on in his head. "Mister Tilman, I heard you and Mister Ward talking," James at last volunteered quietly. "I don't like him either."

"Why's that, son?" Suddenly Tilman was all ears.

"When he talks to my mother he's real polite, but when she's not around, he ignores me or he yells at me. I saw a little boy downtown run into Mister Ward on the sidewalk, and Mister Ward swatted him and called him a bad word."

Tilman exchanged looks with Butter.

"Mister Dan didn't like him, neither. Sometimes Mister Dan would take me to town with him and buy me a licorice whip or a bottle of pop. One day Mister Ward and another man talked mean to Dan, but they didn't see me. I was playing in the hayloft. The other man sounded like little bells when he walked."

"What were they talking about, James?" Tilman asked gently.

"I don't know. Mister Ward just wanted Mister Dan to tell him when the stage was coming, I guess. They were mean, and I got scared. Mister Ward had a gun so I put my hands over my ears."

He looked like he was about to start crying.

"Well James, what did your mama say when you told her?"

"I didn't tell her. I was afraid she'd be upset if I did, and start crying again."

"James, you're a good boy. Why don't you get down from there and bring us some coffee, okay?"

After he'd scampered off, Butter and Tilman walked back outside, and Butter said, "Right smart young 'un. That Ward's one of them two I tol' you about, runs the town."

"Butter, why would Ward want to know a stage schedule?

They're listed on a flyer at the station. It doesn't make sense for Ward to brace Dan with a pistol drawn over a schedule time, for Dan was never one to carry a short gun. And who was that other fellow siding Ward?" Tilman asked. "Maybe Sheriff would know." Going for days with nothing to help find the killer, Tilman thought to himself, and now all this, and from a little boy. "If he's in on Dan's death, then Mister Ward's going to be shaking hands with the devil."

James brought two tin cups of strong coffee, looking down and walking carefully so none spilled. Butter sat down in the shade, groaned with pleasure, and leaned back against the side of a boulder. The valley before them looked clean and new under the clear blue sky, with a few fair weather clouds down low in the south around the Sangre de Cristo Mountains, mares' tails curving through the sky way up high to the north. There was much to think about this day. Tilman decided it might be a good idea to ride into town to look at Mister Bill Ward's place when evening came.

"Butter, answer me another question. After all you've seen you still believe what the preacher said is true?"

Butter turned and looked at Tilman, surprised at the change of subject.

"You think it's not some happy-ending pap, some pie-in-the-sky-by-and-by bedtime story?"

Butter leaned back and closed his eyes, and waited so long to answer Tilman thought he was being ignored.

"Tilman, when my pappy died, I quit school in the fourth grade to help out round home. I got no way of proving it one way or the other. I can't look at this world 'thout I believe there's a plan behind it all. I see the sun by day an' the moon by night, an' all them stars, an' I see the seasons a-changin'—they ain't no accident. I got no education to explain what I'm seein'. I'm a simple man with only my faith," he said, patting his left chest with a calloused hand, "an' I believe from here." He watched Tilman closely. "I'd hate t' think this here is all there is, that when I go under there's only nothin' for all eternity."

"Why, Butter, you've the soul of a poet!" Tilman joked.

"Here," he said, "I said I ain't got much education. I didn't say I was stupid."

Shouted hello's drew the two men's attention to the road from town. Turning into the drive to Catherine's house were a magnificent green-lacquered open phaeton pulled by a pair of high-stepping matched grays, followed by two horse-drawn work carriages packed with laughing men and women. Catherine's guests hurried to greet the newcomers, with many good-natured catcalls and hoots flying back and forth.

"Hot dang," Butter said as he stood and stretched, "here comes the 'town ball' team from Colorado Springs. Call them the 'Reds.' They played a team of miners from California Gulch yesterday, beat 'em seven t' nought."

"And they've come here to celebrate?"

"Reckon so," Butter said, "but a couple of the Yankee boys come to the valley here after the war used to play back east—they claim they was good enough to be in one of them big clubs in New York, and so they throwed down a challenge. We're gonna have us a game of what they call 'base ball' here."

"I never played it, myself," Tilman said.

"I done it some," Butter laughed, "but knowed right off it's a young man's game. We'll watch it some an' I'll tell you what I know 'bout it, which won't take long a-tall."

They laughed. While the ladies gathered up the little remaining food, a few of the men laid out bats, balls and soft leather mitts while others marked off the bases. When everything seemed to be in order they struck up a lively "base ball" game out in the pasture behind the barn. The Reds had a small but loud cheering section made up of young ladies clustered around the man who arrived in the phaeton. Tilman figured the women were players' wives.

The Mahonville players, captained by a big Irish cook from one of the valley ranches, called themselves the Green Nine and were cheered loudly by the locals.

Gathered in the shade near Tilman and Butter, the musicians ignored the game as they picked and sang some lively music Tilman recognized from the Appalachians, soon attracting their own small gathering of admirers. Sarah would have loved it. But for all the homey peacefulness around them, Tilman had questions unanswered, and his mind was uneasy. That pastor, what did he know he wasn't telling? And Catherine, just how involved with Ward was she?

Chapter Twelve

The day drifted into sunny mid-afternoon, a languid, easy peacefulness for men with stomachs full. The Colorado Springs ball team soundly trounced the local boys in a good-natured match, and the musicians had drifted away to watch the end of the game. The camaraderie of the day belied the grimness beneath the glitter of the nearby town. James left his shoes by the creek and ran barefoot to play hide and seek with some other boys. Butter grumbled off to sleep in the porch swing up at the house, his curly gray beard resting on his chest.

Alone, Tilman leaned back on the trunk of a shady willow tree tilted low over the creek, his hat tugged low over his eyes. Drowsily, he watched as Catherine quietly lent a hand putting away the leftovers, or stopped to give a kind word where needed. As families gathered all their things together, she waved them off, laughing and lightly hugging the women-folk as they climbed into their wagons. She was the picture of a woman who loved people and was happiest when help-ing others. Tilman saw her slip extra leftovers to some of the families that had too many children hanging over the wagon sides, or to mothers that looked ten years older than they should have. These were women worn out early from years of one child after another, no end in sight, and only their love for their families keeping them going. Catherine caught one of the last wagons, ran back into the house and returned carrying a big jar of medicinal herbs. Tilman had seen her dosing James with her homemade tea brewed from those herbs when he was coughing in the early morning a few days before. The wagon disappeared down the road as she waved and then paused to watch a yellow and black butterfly.

Pastor Fry came over and sat down and stretched out his legs, sighing. "Saw you and Ward before the service." He smiled. "Thought you two roosters were going to have at it right here."

"What's on your mind, Pastor?" Tilman didn't need some preacher reminding him of the fool he had almost made of himself.

"I need to tell you something that may help. A year or so ago I was tending the flocks in a mining town over by Durango. There was a big fellow I saw around the camps, kind of reminded me of this Bill Ward. Wore a full beard, a rough customer, I gathered, though I never had any truck with him. His pard was one of the nastiest people I ever saw. Doubt he ever got near soap and a razor. Nasty disposition too."

He had Tilman's full attention, but where was this story leading?

"Him and his pard disappeared from the camps about the same time somebody pulled off a pretty lucrative high-grading scheme. You know what that is?"

Tilman shook his head. "I've heard a little, but tell me more." Tilman wanted the man to keep on talking.

"Well, up at the mines they separate the ores by grade. The high grade is the best of course; it's the kind of stuff that can bring up to eighty dollars a ton or more, and that includes almost pure gold from a vein. It's separated from everything else. The mine tally boss will record it in his book and store it at the mine in an unused drift until they have enough to ship off to the stamp mill. Sometimes they'll also store bags of placer gold in there and ship it too. The company freighters will haul it down the mountain. A big high-grade scheme will have an inside man or two, and after the tally boss is done—he don't usually come back and check once he's done—they'll switch the bags of high-grade ore with some ordinary stuff, and then in the middle of the night, slug the night watchman and haul the good stuff off. They'll have an assayer on the payroll that'll process it for them. Nobody suspects an assayer because they process ore samples all the time. He'll know how to get rid of it to make a fine profit for everybody. Mostly they do it a little at a time. But the one I'm talking about made off with a whole burro train of pretty rich stuff, and one of the guards turned up dead. The other one was never seen again, probably in on the deal." He pulled up his knees and rubbed them. "They went up the mountain behind the camp, but it snowed that night and it covered their tracks."

Everything he said tallied with what Skinny Morris had said.

"Ward?"

"Can't say for sure, but I got a feeling. Was I you I'd sure be careful. There's lots of opportunity around here, what with the way ores are moved, and how the placer dust is shipped on the treasure stage." He studied Tilman carefully. "Opportunity won't last long with the railroad coming. That'll all change. Anybody planning a move would want to be done before they hit town."

"You must've been *some* horse soldier." Tilman grinned, standing and stretching. "Glad we never crossed paths."

"Me too. You ever hear what happens to cavalry dumb enough to charge infantry?"

Tilman walked up to the porch where Catherine met him with a glass of iced lemonade and invited him to visit with her. They sat in cushioned white wicker chairs at the opposite end of the porch from Butter.

"It's been a long time since I went to a church picnic like this." Tilman sipped the lemonade. "Good folks to be around. Most of my time is spent with the other kind these days. A man forgets."

"What happened between you and Bill this morning?"

On guard, Tilman figured he'd best be careful here. She didn't hide what was on her mind. "Oh, we had a little disagreement."

"About what?" she insisted.

"You."

"Do I have to drag it out of you, Tilman?" A slight blush told him she was a little hot under the collar.

"Seems like he figures to own you, and he kind of wants me to ride on back to Texas. He got pushy about it, and I don't cotton to being told what to do by anybody, particularly a man I just met." Tilman didn't think she needed to know about the threat he'd made. He still couldn't say for sure Ward had anything to do with Dan's death. For sure he's not one to trust, nor did Tilman want anyone telling him what he'd been thinking. Would she tell him?

"You've got him all wrong. Why, when he comes calling he's a perfect gentleman." Her voice got steadily louder. "You have no right to run him off like you did. Mister Ward is part owner of a bank and is one of our most prominent citizens. Besides, he's working hard to get the county seat moved from Granite to Mahonville so we can be a more respectable town. He's our strongest booster to get the name of the town changed to Vista Buena, which he says is Spanish for 'beautiful view.' "

"I suppose next he'll want to get himself elected mayor."

"Yes, he will, and I dare say he'll make a good one. We want a town where it's safe to bring up children and for respectable women to walk the streets without fear of being molested. Why, he has plans to improve the road across Cottonwood Pass for supplying the mines at Tin Cup, and make our town the most civilized in the valley. He even has plans for a theatre to bring in actors from as far away as New York, or Paris!"

"You choose to see him as a fine gentleman with your best interests at heart. I see him differently, for what he really is—the devil in disguise." All at once for some reason it was very important that he make her see Ward for the kind of man he really was. She was too good a woman to fall for his lies. She was too trusting!

"Why do you think that Pastor Fry and I are the only ones who'll stay at your boardinghouse these days? Ward runs them all off with threats! Did you know that?" Tilman clenched his fists with frustration. "He threatened Dan and he threatened me, ordering me to move out. Any other time or place and I'd have called him out for that!" Tilman drew closer to Catherine, unaware of how he might be scaring her. "And what about the drunk that molested you in town, that Shorty? He's one of Bill's boys. That's the kind of man he wants close to him. Aren't you seeing only what he wants you to see? Why can't you see beyond that?" Tilman demanded hotly. "Can't you see I am trying to protect you?" Wanting to stand between her and danger, Tilman felt compelled to try to reason with her.

Before he could react, she was out of her chair, her face mirroring the fear her soul must feel at the thought of making such a terrible mistake in judgment.

"Tilman Wagner! What right do you have to want to protect me? Did I ask for help?" She was just warming up. Catherine stood toe to toe with Tilman, the sides of her hair falling out of the neat clasp she normally kept it tied up in. "Do you really think that the devil is here in this town? And anyway," she paused as Tilman stepped back against the porch railing, "how can there be a devil, Tilman, if there is no God?" Her eyes iced over. "Just how do you of all people explain that?" She grabbed a leftover plate from the porch table, huffed to herself, and slammed the front door as she went into the house. Her frustration with Tilman and what he'd said was evident with each step she took!

"Well, pard," came an amused voice from under Butter's hat, "sounds like you've wore yore welcome thinner than the seat of a pair of last year's cheap britches."

"Hey, Butter," Tilman said, taking off his hat and wiping off the sweatband. "I'd no right to say those things. Sorry, but I forgot you were sleeping. Guess I woke you and made Catherine angry all in one try. I feel bad, and I guess I ought to go apologize. I'll never understand women." He couldn't help but admire the way she had stood up for Ward, even though he knew she was dead wrong. She would be quite an ally to have on a person's side.

"Ain't a dang one of us ever will. No sir, let her think about what you said. It needed sayin' an' she needed to hear it, so if she's smart as I think, she'll figure it out." He sat up with a grunt and stretched. "What say you and me take a couple of days, mebbe do a little fishin'. A man just naturally needs some time to hisself now an' ag'in. I got a place I like to go where a body can walk around in his long handles, holler an' cuss an' spit an' not be concerned 'bout anybody or anything."

"Well, why ain't we there yet?"

"Get your traps together and come on down to the station by first light and we'll head out."

Tilman needed to distance himself from the town and from Catherine so he could think.

Chapter Thirteen

Tilman and Butter pulled out early on a cold, autumn morning, soon after the sun rose into a bright, cloudless sky. Catherine hadn't appeared, but she had left hot coffee and rolls and a sack lunch for the men. Maybe she wasn't too mad, after all. Butter wanted to show Tilman some things along the way to the lakes up on the northern edge of the county. Instead of following the stage road out of town, they took the unfinished rail bed across the Arkansas, passing near the workers' tent camp. Many of the workers were Chinese, squatting around breakfast fires, deftly eating rice with chopsticks. They stopped to stare in silence as the two riders came near. A guard, armed with a Winchester, got up from his chair near a shed and gave Tilman and Butter a hard look. Satisfied that the two were no threat, the guard returned to his seat.

When Tilman and Butter reached a place where a dry stream bed dropped to the Arkansas, Butter said they were at Four Mile Creek, and turned his horse aside to lead the way up a steep, rocky slope on the east side of the valley. After a climb of several hundred feet, Tilman was glad his paloose was mountain-bred, for it was rough going. The higher they rode the cooler the still morning air became. The sharp smell of pinon pines filled the air. They reached a level place, free of trees, which was actually an exposed slab of granite near the creek bed. Butter and Tilman dismounted and walked to a curious, unnatural circular cut, several feet in diameter, in the granite rock. Butter's knees popped as he squatted on his haunches by a place that looked like a donut had been cut out of the stone, and it was about a foot deep.

"People been taking gold out of these hills for many a year," Butter explained. "Folks tell me Spaniards used this place to grind and wash ore dug out where the creek over there comes down off this here Free Gold Hill."

"Morris told me about the stamp mill they're building down by the river," Tilman said. "Was this sort of like that?"

"You might say so," Butter replied. "Back in them days, they'd use a burro, maybe a man if they had no critter, walking around pushin' a pole, what you'd call a 'muller,' to turn a grind stone 'round the mortar, the flat rock here."

"Butter, I've seen something like that. Back home that's how we used to grind sugar cane stalks to make molasses!"

"It's sort of the same." He chuckled.

They mounted up and headed back down the hill.

"Folks say the Spaniards took a lot of gold out of these mountains."

Tilman braced for another of Butter's stories; how that man loved to hear himself talk! But his stories usually had a good teaching point, and they were entertaining, and they passed the time. Tilman's family was not much for writing, so everything was passed from generation to generation by telling stories. Wagner family gatherings were educational, especially when Tilman's uncle talked about making corn liquor up the holler. While Tilman enjoyed good conversation as well as the next man, he had always liked to read too, so he usually had one or two books tucked into his saddlebags. Books were hard to come by around Mahonville—that tells you a lot about a place—and both the local newspapers tended to either toe the political party line chosen by the owner or else wallow in gossip and hearsay.

Butter got tired of waiting for Tilman to take his cue to ask a question about Spanish gold, so after aiming a sharp look at Tilman he continued his tale.

"There was a lot of Utes around in those days. One time a pack train hauling gold to Santa Fe was attacked by a Ute war party down near the Chalk Cliffs south of here. They hid the gold, and it was ever' man for hisself." Butter laughed. "Now, that's just a story, for I don't know who was left to tell it. I wonder, were the Utes after the gold or just out to kill the Spaniards? No tellin'. Maybe the gold's still there." He rambled on. "I hear there's gold buried at the Rabbit Ears, on the Santa Fe Trail cutoff down in New Mexico Territory, but don't it sound an awful lot like the same story as here? A pack train ambushed by Indians, the Spaniards bury the gold and scatter. Sounds mighty suspicious to me. Folks always want to believe there's easy money to be had, if you're lucky enough."

"You don't believe the tales?"

"When I first come here, back in the late fifties, time of the first gold rush, I seen fellers a-usin' grind stones to bust ore. Weren't Spaniards, neither. Seems to me the stories of Spanish treasure is just wishful talk."

When they reached the bottom of the hill, they found some shallow water that was not too rocky, and so they forded the river and continued north. The morning sun warmed their backs as they rode up the valley. At a place where the land became generally level and clear of trees and scrub brush for several miles, Butter said, "Round here folks call this Five Elks, all the way to the river. Got something else I want to show you," Butter said. Off to the right and across the river he pointed out the stage road from Mahonville to Granite and Leadville.

"Last week I brought my stage on a run up the valley an' I seen a man out here target shootin' with a long gun. He was firin' from a prone position at a man-sized target a long ways away, oh, I figure maybe half a mile. They'd put up a small tent, like a Sibley, but the sides rolled up, like it was a holiday. Tent had a little red pennant on it. They had chairs and an umbrella, real comfortable." Butter watched Tilman closely as he talked. "Another man was marking the target. They was too far away for me to know who they were, but one of their horses picketed nearby was a fine looking pinto."

They dismounted at a place where the grass was flattened. Butter said, "This is where the tent was, and up yonder was the firing line." Tilman started to look around. There wasn't much to see, for someone had carefully picked up all the expended brass cartridge cases. Tilman saw a glint of light in the grass and found, pressed into a footprint in the dirt, a spent .50 caliber cartridge case. He picked it up to study it. Morris found a similar case after Dan was killed, the one Tilman now carried in his vest. He pulled Morris's cartridge from his pocket and compared it to the one he'd just found. The firing pin mark on the primer in the cartridge base was the same on both brass cases, and Tilman could see where the gun's cartridge extractor had left scratches on the cases. Tilman held them up in the light and saw that both cartridge cases showed the same kind of scratches, and they seemed to match. The lip of each of the brass cases was bent slightly out of round in the same way where they had struck the face of the breech as the cases were ejected after firing.

"Butter, do all Sharps leave the same marks on a cartridge case?" Tilman asked.

"Danged if I know."

"My holster gun is a Colt .45, and my waist gun is too. Why don't we test fire both, and we'll compare firing pin marks on the case primer caps."

After firing one shot from each of his pistols, Tilman ejected the empty brass from each gun and compared the cases of the spent rounds. The small indentations on the primers were different in size and placement on the cap, even though each was a Colt .45.

"We're going to have to find us another Sharps big .50 and shoot it so we can compare the cases," he said to Butter. Tilman wondered if this shooter was the man who killed Dan. He'd sure like to find him and talk to him. They walked downrange to where the targets had been and found a paper silhouette target, crumbled and caught on an elk horn cactus. Spreading it out, Tilman found nine bullet holes so closely grouped in the center of the chest area of the target he could have covered them with the palm of his hand. There was one hole low and to the left. Tilman figured that the one shot thrown out must be a fluke, looking at the accuracy of the other shots. Whoever he was, that man could shoot.

Now Tilman could see why Butter wanted him to ride up this road. Butter was out to show Tilman something, even if he was going at it in a roundabout way. Why didn't he come right out and tell Tilman? Whoever it was shooting out here, Tilman thought he'd sure hate to be caught under the fellow's gun. He's not the kind to miss. Tilman had hoped to get a chance to think about Catherine, stubborn woman that she was, but now he'd learned something that may help find Dan's killer, so he'd just have to worry about her later. Since they still had some distance to ride, Tilman could only guess that Butter had still more he wanted Tilman to see.

Chapter Fourteen

"I was thinking," Butter said, breaking the long silence since they'd left Five Elks, "Le'me tell you this. I seen Army sharpshooters training that a-way. I knowed some of 'em. They was generally a standoffish bunch, kept to themselves, and nobody much liked them. I hate a sharpshooter worser'n I hate a rattlesnake, an' I hate the dickens out of a rattler."

"Who were you with in the war, Butter?"

"The Forty-eighth Alabama, Law's Brigade. You?"

"Pettigrew's Brigade, Twenty-sixth North Carolina. We both fought under ol' Pete Longstreet. Butter, you went in on my right on the second day at Gettysburg."

"Reckon I did. We got whupped that day . . . whupped bad. Many a good man was shot down on that field. The Yankees cotched me about dark when I was so wore out it was all I could do to stand. I was about to perish for a drink of water."

Tilman watched as tears came to Butter's eyes, and listened in awe as he began an almost unbelievable tale of his experiences on long ago battlefields. As he spoke his voice became thick, and he paused often to take a deep breath. It was almost as if he were reliving the moments. Butter's hands shook, and Tilman noticed he rested them on his saddle horn, to hide the motion. Butter continued.

"The sun was unmerciful hot that July day at Gettysburg in 1863." If the Confederate Army could get around the Union left, then Longstreet's Corps would roll up the Yankee lines and there was a good chance to win the war right then and there. Butter's brigade, as a part of Longstreet's Corps, had just marched more than fifteen miles to arrive on the field. "Reckon much of it was at the double quick in the midday heat so we could get in position to attack," Butter recalled.

Tilman knew that the Union Army left had been anchored on two low hills called the Round Tops. When Butter told it, Tilman could picture in his mind's eye when and where Ol' Pete stopped to dress their ranks before they crossed the Emmitsburg Pike, and to give the boys a chance to catch their breath before attacking. Butter said, "My feet was cut and bleedin' for, like many of the boys, I was without shoes since we'd left Virginia. Our throats were parched and canteens dry, and we wasn't to organize a party to collect and fill canteens for a taste of cool water."

Butter paused to watch as a bald eagle, a fish gripped in its talons, flew past heading for its nest. He continued, "My younger brother George took his squad's canteens and, without orders, ran down to a nearby spring to fill them. As I watched, George knelt and pushed aside some cattails to fill one of the canteens in the shallow water. Of a sudden, I seen George jerked upright, struck by a bullet that killed him instantly. He fell face down in the water. I heard the sound of that shot an' I hollered but it weren't no use, my voice was lost in the noise of skirmish fire and shouting that broke out all along both sides of the line. Before I could help little brother, the colonel called out, 'Up, boys, we're going in.' and the sergeants moved the lines out into the open field that led to the Emmitsburg Pike where the Yankee Army was digging rifle pits in a farmer's peach orchard.

"The day after I was captured I learned that the Yankee skirmishers facing our lines had been Berdan's Regiment of Sharpshooters, all of them crack shots, all armed with seven-shot Burnside repeatin' rifles. The Yankees talked freely, braggin' about the battle, and how the Johnnies' attack had been shot to pieces."

Tilman thought back to those times, that fearful day and place. It began as momentous events often do, with a seemingly insignificant incident, and the Yankees gloried in the telling of it. Tilman had heard several versions of what went on that hot afternoon, but most of the stories agreed it was generally like this: There was a widow lived in a shack on the lower end of Seminary Ridge where Longstreet's men waited to begin the attack, and the widow had a curious young son. Naturally, the boy came out of the house to look at the first Rebels he had ever had a chance to see. All around his home were thousands of Confederate infantry, drawn up in lines of battle, several ranks deep, lying at rest on their polished Enfield rifles. The Rebels called to the boy to bring a bucket of water from the well, and one wag told him to bring a washtub full if he could tote one, but the boy was frozen in place with fear. Then, disobeying his mother's pleading admonition to come in the house where it was safe, the boy panicked and ran. Leaving the woods like a spooked rabbit, he crossed a wheat field and ran through the Yankee skirmish line where a quick-thinking soldier finally tackled the boy. Breathlessly he told the soldiers what he had seen. Someone took him to find Hiram Berdan, and the wide-eyed, frightened boy told the colonel, "There's Rebs in the woods yonder. Laying in rows." Berdan sent one of his scouts, a man named Seth, a former mountain man from the Rockies, a man who fancied a buckskin shirt, to see if the boy was telling the truth. Seth came close to the woods that concealed the Rebels, and lay down behind a low stone wall to watch. He saw a single soldier in a homespun butternut uniform step out of the woods carrying several canteens and hurry to a spring in some low ground. When the Reb laid his rifle down and knelt to fill the canteens, Berdan's man killed him. The Yankees made Seth out to be a hero for killing the first Rebel along that part of the line, and they laughed as battle-hardened soldiers will, about how the Reb jumped when struck by the ball.

Butter had heard the same accounts, but went on to say, "I always felt that wasn't a part of the battle, for it had not properly started yet. I believe it was little more than murder. Anyhow, it come on to evening of the last day of the battle, there was a right hot cavalry fight a-goin' on behind the lines near where us prisoners was being gathered, and the guards panicked and some commenced to runnin' away. In all the noise, smoke, and confusion with bullets a-flyin' and of course it bein' almost dark, I was able to slip away from the guards. That's when I started to hate sharpshooters. Not Yankees, lemme say, but sharpshooters."

Butter continued his story. "Much later on we was at Spotsylvania Court House, it was May of '64, and I remember how once again the sun was as hot as any July day. My regiment was in reserve behind a place where the trenches bent toward the Federal lines. We called it the Mule Shoe Salient, but the Yankees came to call it the Bloody Angle, for we shot down a many of 'em right there. I watched while a sharpshooter, one of our boys, a-carryin' a special made Enfield rifle—you know, one of them with a heavy reinforced barrel and one of them new telescopic sights as long as the barrel itself—slung his rifle and climbed into the lower branches of a hickory tree. One of the boys told me the sharpshooter had orders to find and shoot Yankee officers, and sure enough, later that day he fired one shot. That night word spread along the lines that a sharpshooter had killed Union General 'Uncle' John Sedgwick, a man well thought of by his boys."

After the war, I read a newspaper story wrote by Sedgwick's aide, a Major Hyde. It said the general was shot while he was a-talkin' with an artillery battery commander a half-mile from the Confederate lines at Bloody Angle. Hyde wrote that he had just warned the general about sharpshooters being active, but said the general had only laughed, and told him, 'They couldn't hit an elephant at this distance.' No sooner had he spoken the last words than a bullet struck him in the face just below his left eye, an' killed him instantly.

"I'll never know for sure if I saw the sharpshooter that killed Sedgwick," Butter said, "but it was possibly the same man who climbed the tree behind me that day at Spotsylvania."

It was as if things bottled up for years deep in the old man's heart had finally found escape. Butter kept on talking. "It was durin' the fightin' around Petersburg, Virginia, in 1864, we was all of us, Yank and Reb alike, pretty much in agreement in hatin' sharpshooters. Matter of fact we'd talk about it when we'd meet at night to trade tobacco for coffee between the battle lines. Us boys'd reached an informal truce among ourselves, so that we'd call out "Down, Yank!" or "Watch it, Reb!" when an officer made us get up and shoot. The boys had simply seen enough killin'. Sharpshooters ignored such truces, so when one was killed, why, you'd hear cheers all up and down the trench lines. Most men come to think that style of killin' was too much like murder, catchin' a man unaware, even when he was a-steppin' behind a bush to do his business. I'm som'at kinder now in my later years, so folks say, but I still dislike them men who killed unsuspectin' soldiers from hidey holes." Butter laughed, and said, "I hope God'll be patient with me while I work on forgiving those people. I figure it might take me a while longer to get her done, and hope I'll live long enough to see it."

As Tilman listened to Butter, he finally came to understand. This was Butter's way of explaining why he had such strong feelings of anger for the man who'd killed his friend, Tilman's son, Dan. He understood too that as of now he was not alone in hunting the killer. Butter, without saying it in so many words, was siding him and had chosen Tilman to be his friend. It was his way of telling Tilman what he needed to know about him. Now Tilman had a friend he could count on, a steady, dependable, battle-tested friend who knew what could happen, and was not afraid to risk his life. Butter did this, not for Tilman, not for a fellow Confederate soldier, but for Dan. It made Tilman see Butter differently now, a man sure of his beliefs, certain in his faith, one not afraid to risk his life for or with a friend.

"Butter, why didn't you tell me it was you who sent the telegram about Dan?"

"Well sir, I needed to know what kind of a man you really were. I figgered Dan came from good stock, and now I know for sure."

Was Tilman worthy of Butter's friendship? Tilman hoped he would measure up and never put the man in danger.

Chapter Fifteen

Near Granite the stage road followed close beside the river. Rounding a bend, they came upon a man staggering along, and their first impression was that it was a drunk. However, as they rode closer, it was plain to see the man had been badly beaten. One eye was swollen shut, and his lower lip was split, as was his scalp above the swollen eye. His wounds were fresh, still bleeding, and his hair matted with drying blood. This was shaping up to be an interesting day! Quickly tying off the horses, Butter sat the man down and began to clean his injuries.

"What happened?" Tilman asked. "Who did this?"

"Claim jumpers," the man said, dabbing at the cut on his lip with a rag. "Two fellows just rode up and told me to light a shuck. Said I was on their claim. No such a thing. I filed on that claim legal and proper up at the courthouse."

"Where's your claim?" Butter asked.

"Just up yonder," the man answered, wincing as he began pointing upriver, "by that bend where the gravelly point bar sticks out. You can see it from here."

"This happens a lot around here," Butter explained. "They'll run a man off his mining claims, and even in town, why, they'll jump city lots. Bold fellers, just move in and squat, and claim it's their'n."

As he spoke six grim-faced miners climbed up from the riverbank to see what was going on.

"Dutchy," they asked their friend, "what's the trouble?"

"They jumped my claim!" Dutchy painfully explained.

"These fellows here?"

The gathered miners became uneasy, casting threatening looks at Butter and Tilman.

"No," Dutchy replied, "they're down yonder on my claim."

The men were quick to anger at the plight of their friend and scrambled back to their cabins to get rifles, shotguns, and pistols—one even had an axe. They were a rugged group, ready to take matters into their own hands, and somebody was likely to be dead soon if they stormed into their friend's camp to take on the claim jumpers.

"Butter, you've got a rope on your saddle," Tilman stated, "so let's help these boys."

Riding the short distance to the plundered claim, leading the band of irate miners, Tilman and Butter were approaching the claim as two men stepped out to meet them.

"You just keep on a-ridin', you ain't welcome on our claim!" one shouted, shifting his coat to reveal a pistol in his waistband by way of backing his bold talk.

"That's the one done this to me," the injured Dutchy said, standing beside Tilman's horse. "He pistol-whipped me."

The band of hardcase miners spread out to surround the claim jumpers, who suddenly realized that by all odds they might not live to see the sun set tonight. The "click-click" sounds of gun hammers being cocked seemed loud in the sudden quiet. Guns were leveled at the thieves, and the miner with the shotgun strode forward to put the barrels against one man's belly. A single wrong move and men would instantly be blown into eternity, and the jumpers knew it.

"Butter, string the rope over that big limb on the sycamore

tree yonder," Tilman called. Turning to his new mining friends, Tilman smiled. "Boys, take their guns, and tie their hands."

"Hot dang!" someone shouted. "A necktie party!"

"No, mister, please, we ain't done nothing," the mean one begged.

"Oh, what's going to happen to my poor wife and baby?" the other one cried.

Butter quickly rigged a noose on the dangling rope and dabbed the end around Tilman's saddle horn and the fun began. "Take that one first." Tilman pointed to the thief who'd challenged him.

The rope was quickly dropped over the claim jumper's head and snugged tight around his neck. Tilman nudged his horse, backing him a few steps to take the slack out of the rope and lift the man to his toes.

"Claim jumper!" someone taunted.

"Shake hands with the devil and tell him your friend's on his way!" called another.

Tilman held the horse in place, steady and unmoving.

"Can you smell that brimstone, mister?" a grinning miner asked, jabbing at the man with his rifle butt. "Can you feel that heat?"

Butter watched Tilman closely, unsure of the Texan's next move.

Tilman wouldn't go any further with the hanging, but it was a sure way to teach these boys a lesson. The miners would simply have lynched them on the spot, but Tilman knew that if he interceded, then the two men might have a chance to live.

"All right," Tilman said as the man's feet touched the ground. Butter stepped close and loosened the rope.

"Neck-stretching, Colorado style, boys. Get it?" Butter said.

"Boys, let's have them boots and socks," Butter called, "shirts and pants while you're at it."

While the claim jumpers stripped down to their long-handled underwear, Butter and Tilman watched as the miners crowded close. A few solid kicks were delivered for good measure.

The miners were mostly an honest, hard-working group of men come to scratch a living from the earth under the most difficult conditions. Pick and shovel work in icy water made them lean and hard-muscled. A weak man couldn't stand up to the rigors of the life and was soon weeded out. Few miners ever struck it rich, and most eked out a bare living while sending most of their earnings to the folks back home. They tended to look out for each other, and were not the kind of men to take being pushed around without fighting back. The claim jumpers whimpered, mincing around barefoot on the rough gravel roadbed with lots of "Ouch!" and "Oh, that smarts!"

"You start walking and don't stop until you're out of this county," the miner with the shotgun said, "and if we ever see you around here again, you're liable to be shot like a hydrophoby dog!"

"Git."

The two dejected, beaten men, dressed only in their long underwear, took off in a shambling trot. The would-be thieves were barely fifty yards off when a shotgun thundered, rock salt spattering the retreating backsides. Squalling, the claim jumpers disappeared at a dead run around the bend, chased by the derisive laughter of the miners.

"Old Cicero had him a watermelon patch by his shack," one man said by way of explanation, "and he made up some rock salt loads to keeps fellers from raiding his melons!"

"Dutchy," the miners said to their injured friend, "whatever's in their pockets is yours. Fair pay for your hurts."

"Thanks, boys," and turning to Butter and Tilman, he said, "I'm much obliged to you both."

As they rode into Granite, Tilman said to Butter, "Back in Texas we'd call this a quiet morning, just an ordinary day."

Butter smiled, suddenly serious. "Them miners would've killed those two if you hadn't done what you did."

"Maybe Pastor Fry's talking is getting to me." Tilman spoke Pastor Fry's name, but he knew it was Catherine's doing. "Anyway, a killing was uncalled for. I'm glad we happened along. Over there's the place where I found Bat Masterson. Let's go see if he knows anything about that sharpshooter."

The saloon was as crowded, smelly, and as noisy as ever. Butter waited by the door. Tilman pushed to the bar, said "Shot of rye," at the barkeep's raised eyebrows, then asked if Bat Masterson was around.

"Bat's gone to Leadville," the man replied, "don't expect he'll be coming back this way." As he spoke his eyes shifted, and Tilman turned to see two hard-looking men come in. They were both tall, well dressed, and wore badges. They were looking at Tilman and one asked the other, "Is he the one from Texas?"

They didn't sugarcoat it. "You have one hour to get out of town," the older of the two said, "I'll not have gunplay in my town."

"No trouble, just looking to find the man who killed my son."

When Tilman explained, the lawmen listened intently to the part about the long shot across the river, and then relaxed.

"People have been talking about a man doing some long-range target shooting south of town," the young deputy said.

"That's over in Chaffee County," his boss said, "and out of our jurisdiction. Finish your drink, and drift."

Dropping a dollar on the bar for the drink he never touched, Tilman drifted. Word was getting around about that mysterious shooter. It had to tie in with Dan's death, somehow. Did Butter know Bat had already gone to Leadville? Maybe Bat even made the trip on the stage driven by Butter! How much more did Butter know?

"Butter, I've got some questions I want to ask you."

Butter smiled, but said nothing.

Chapter Sixteen

Mid-afternoon found Tilman and Butter on a well traveled trail about two miles below the mining town of Dayton which, according to talk, was enjoying a new silver mining boom. They followed a new road on the north side of the lower lake at Twin Lakes. A group of Cache Creek placer miners, wanting more water to compete with the hydraulikers, was busily throwing up a dam across the valley to enlarge the lower lake. Tilman stopped to talk. They'd built a series of cofferdams to divert the runoff while they raised and filled sections of the dam, and it was almost time to blast out the last coffer and complete the dam. Things moved quickly around this part of Colorado, for the miners pointed out that a Swiss fellow had already built a brand new resort hotel, the Interlaken, on the south shore to take advantage of the lake view in front of the mountains.

"Some Dayton people don't like what we've done and were threatening to blow up the dam," one of the Cache Creek boys said, "but when the 'Old Pirate' sided with us, why, we heard no more of that."

Another laughed. "Said he was going to mount a thirty-two pounder on a gig, sail around the point and bombard the town. They believed him!"

"That's 'Beat' for you!" Butter hooted, slapping his thigh. "Be seein' you, boys."

Riding toward the settlement, Butter said, "He's my friend, Zebulon Mansfield is, an' lots of folks call him 'Old Pirate' and you'll soon see why."

They turned in at the yard of a long, low, log construction having many parts, a hotel of sorts. Tilman looked twice at the sternly formidable, tall man on the porch waiting to greet them. While he was not a pirate like a person would expect to see in a drawing in *Frank Leslie's Weekly Magazine,* with a peg leg and eye patch and brandishing a cutlass, Zebulon Mansfield stood on that porch every inch a ship's master on the quarterdeck of his sailing vessel.

"Come alongside, shipmate!" his voice boomed at Butter.

"Howdy, Beat," Butter answered, swinging down from the saddle, grinning as he introduced Tilman.

Stepping close to shake hands, Tilman found the man's grip was strong. He sized up the sailor and saw a man about fifty, with gray hair and a full beard, with dark eyes staring from under bushy brows. His skin was burned a deep brown from years on the open sea. As seagulls are sometimes blown far inland by a storm, this man, so different from others who lived in Colorado, must have been blown here by life's storms and troubles. Tilman would soon find that was the truth.

"Welcome aboard. Stow your gear, Butter, and then we'll splice the main brace and yarn."

"Aye, sir," Butter responded, pointing out two rooms.

Butter was happier than Tilman had ever seen him. Clearly there was a strong bond of friendship between these two men. The room was clean, if spartan, so Tilman dumped his bedroll and joined Butter and Beat around a table on the porch. An old and wrinkled Chinese man placed a tray with a bottle and glasses on the table in front of the men. He then placed his hands into cuff openings of his shirtsleeves, bowed with a couple of quick bobbing movements of his head, spoke words Tilman didn't understand, then disappeared into the hotel.

"Duck for dinner, boys," Beat said, pouring drinks all around, "you're in for a treat."

Tilman had heard sailors liked rum but he'd never tasted it before, and after one sip decided he hadn't missed much. At last he understood what Mansfield meant by "splice the main brace." Butter relished the fiery liquid, downed his in one swallow and smacked his lips loudly.

Beat turned to Tilman. "Butter, who never set foot on a fine sailing ship, nor even a steam packet, visits me as an excuse to try and reduce my rum stores." He and Butter both laughed at what has obviously become a long-standing joke between two old friends. "What brings you here?"

He listened intently, and by the time Tilman finished telling the story, drink untouched, Mansfield refilled both his own and Butter's glass twice. Leaning back in his chair, Mansfield watched the sun drop behind the rim of steep-sided mountains behind Dayton. He seemed deep in thought.

"Vengeance is an honorable cause," he said.

"I'm not looking for honor."

Mansfield studied Tilman, and read the deep anger that had become Tilman's life in his every move and word. "I meant no offense," he said, "I know the search for revenge, the determination to take an eye for an eye, has a way of consuming a good man, even the most cautious man, burning his soul until there's aught but hate left. In your case, sir, I see that you sit like a man wearing a side arm, ready for action, yet you are not armed."

Tilman started to rise.

"Wait," Mansfield said quietly, "what I have to say may be of some interest to you."

Tilman sat back to listen.

"From the time I left Bedford to sign on as a ship's cabin boy of ten, I sailed the world's seas, learning to fear no man. I fought the sea, the wind, the sun and the darkness, and I fought men in ports around the world. I gloried in it. In fact, rather than avoid fights, I sought them out. I am called Beat because when I served in the Navy some say I was too quick to use the command 'Beat to quarters!' clearing the ship for action, calling out the off-watch, sanding the decks for action.

"I had a son, and I raised him in my image for his mother died in birthing him. He sailed with me, starting as a Boy, Third Class, when he was nine. He grew to be a fine man of twenty years, wise in the ways of the sea and men. We were good men, and strong, and we made our own way, trusting God, our Navy Colts and our cutlasses." The old man paused, remembering.

"I was master of the clipper *Eastern Star.* We were anchored in the stream off the river port of Canton, in China, ready to sail with the morning tide, loaded with fine silks that were all the colors of the rainbow tied up in shimmering pieces of cloth, and exotic teas from the high mountains of China and Tibet worth a king's ransom, and all bound for California. Just at dawn they boarded us, filthy river pirates, swarming over the port rail, our only warning the thump of an oar on the ship's side. The quarterdeck watch sounded the alarm, and Edward, my only son, ever quick to act in an emergency, threw open the small arms locker and led the off-watch to the weather deck.

"The fighting was desperate, hand-to-hand, the worst close quarters kind. I stood by the wheel picking off pirates with my Navy Colts, but I knew their overwhelming numbers were cutting my crew to pieces. Before we could rally, Edward was shot from behind, then clubbed as he fell." He sighed, and sipped his rum.

"I knew he was killed, and we were in danger of losing the ship. I called to the bosun to pull back under my guns. The quartermaster had loaded our two swivel guns—we always mounted them in any foreign port so that we could bear on the gangways and main deck—with triple-shotted canister.

We swept the decks with fire. The effect at that close range was something once seen never forgotten. Hardly a pirate remained standing, and those who did were struck dumb by the carnage, and we quickly dispatched them with pistol and cutlass.

"We threw them over the side, and slipping our anchor cables, drifted toward the sea. Our wounded were taken below to the mess deck to be treated by the ship's doctor.

"Later that day when we were well out to sea, we buried my son as a sailor should be buried, with the shipmates who died with him. We sewed them into mattress covers, each with a cannon shell at his feet. Planks were laid by the rail, one each for Edward and his mates. The crew formed as side-boys, one final time for Edward. I read from the Bible. Then he, with the others, was slipped into the sea as the bosun piped honors, their Earthly troubles ended."

Tilman looked at Butter, and realized that this was why he wanted to come here. Butter was amazing. Turning to Mansfield, Tilman asked, "Do you hate the Chinese?"

"I've given that a lot of thought. No, I don't. I killed those pirates—maybe I was the tool for stopping them from hurting anyone else," he replied. "It's out of my hands. I know they've had to stand accountable for what they did on Earth." He laughed. "We just made sure they stood before their Maker like good sailors reporting to the ship's master at arms for punishment detail. I expect they're burning in eternal fires wherever they are now!

"Mister Wagner, I'm known to speak my mind, and even though we've only just met, I hope you'll still listen. You and I both have lost a son, and we're left behind to suffer. I still have doubts. Did I do all I could to save him? For a time I felt a sense of guilt that I lived and he did not. Why him and not me? I've seen men eaten up with guilt and anger, so that it becomes their whole reason for living. I feel Edward's loss every day of my life, but I believe I did all I could. Now he's with his Maker, and one of these days I'll see him again when the sea gives up her dead."

"You figure there's a heaven and you're going?"

"I do believe that."

"You're saying my only reason for living is my anger?"

"No. You said it. Only you can know that. But, Mister Wagner, why *are* you here?"

Tilman was at a loss. He had worn his anger and need to avenge Dan's death like a badge, and made no bones about it. Yet the man before him had seen and worked with his son every day before he died, but felt no hate for those who took his son away from him. Instead, he looks forward to the day when he's sure he and his son meet again! And Tilman? He'd sent Dan away and then rode all over Texas looking to avenge Sarah's death. Tilman would see Dan maybe once a year. Was he here for revenge or because he felt guilty for sending Dan away?

The men sat in silence in the gathering darkness, each lost to thoughts of distant times and places.

Butter must have been feeling the strong drink for he decided to ease the tension with one of his stories.

"Some old boys I knew back during the war came from down around the Carolina coast. They told me about an English captain sailed out of Beaufort." He pronounced it Bowfort. "On a long voyage, he taken his daughter along, but she took sick and died at sea. Well sir, he wouldn't put her in the sea because she always was afraid of the water, so he put her in a cask of rum and brought her back to Beaufort to be buried!"

"I couldn't do that," Beat said. "A sailor should be buried at sea. It's a sad thing. Edward was the last of our line." Beat looked at Tilman for the first time since he'd started his tale. Then, he smiled, "A rum?" When Tilman declined, he continued.

"I put in at San Francisco, sold my share to the other

owners, and left the sea, like Ulysses," Beat said. "Do you know Homer's tale about Ulysses, Mister Wagner? A Greek sailor of old who, after a ten-year war and another ten years wandering the sea, came home and gave up on the sea. He put an oar over his shoulder and walked inland. He said he'd make his home when he found somebody who'd ask him what to call that thing he was carrying." Beat laughed, and said, "I figure here in the Rockies is far enough from the sea. But, be aware, I find there are other pirates with whom I must contend."

Loud voices raised in argument came from inside the hotel, interrupting the story. Beat went to the door, spoke sternly, and then returned to his seat.

"Stab took one of the ducks and old Wa didn't like it."

Beat looked at Tilman, and then explained. "Wa is my cook, has been for years. Signed on with me on my first trip to Shanghai after our regular cook jumped ship. An old Ute woman called Stab just took up here on her own. Commandeered a shed out back one morning, and that's that. Nobody can pronounce her Ute name. Her people left her to die on a hilltop but some do-gooder Dayton family on a Sunday hiking excursion found her and brought her down. She'd almost starved to death, but she was still game! She tried to stab the man who found her, so we call her Stab."

"He keeps her on to cook fry bread," Butter said, "which this old seadog loves."

"She and Wa fight over the kitchen, and neither will learn the other's language. She evidently admires Wa's queue, and makes scalping motions at the old rascal. He keeps a cleaver handy, even sleeps with it, because he believes he'll never get to heaven without that queue.

"All this land around here used to belong to her tribe, the Utes. From what I'm told, they were powerful, fearsome, and warlike. The Navajo out west of here, themselves known to be fierce fighters, have fought with them for as long as anyone can remember. The Navajos call the Utes

'Bloody Knives.' In return, the Utes refer to the Navajos as 'Skull-Crushers.' "

"If we don't eat soon," Butter complained as he leaned forward and peered toward the dining room, "old Wa's sure to lose another duck!"

Chapter Seventeen

Most of the following day passed with Tilman and Butter down by the lake fishing, and the result was a fine mess of trout. Butter swore there was no finer tasting fish on the planet. He worked hard to get the idea across to Wa that he wanted the fish fried for dinner, but Tilman was sure the Chinese language did not includes words like "cookee" or "fishee" or "chop-chop." Butter was confident that the old cook understood.

Beat announced that some other guests would be arriving later. Charles McRae, a Leadville citizen of some means and something of a womanizer, planned to build his hideaway house on the south shore. "Butter, he's bringing your old friend 'Haw' Tabor to look at some land here as a possible investment. Also, McRae's bringing a couple of ladies with him. They've shipped in oysters, lobster, and champagne on ice, so with your trout we'll have a fine dinner again tonight."

Tilman sat on the porch, his chair tilted back and his boots on the rail, enjoying the warm autumn sunshine with Butter. The more he learned, the more complex and interesting Butter became. Tilman began to think he kept his old 'down-home' accent just to put people off. A man of many acquaintances but few real friends, Tilman needed a friend.

"Butter, who is this fellow Tabor, and how did you come to know him?"

"I used to haul freight for Tabor's store in Leadville. He come here with his wife Augusta and baby Maxcy in 1860, and did some placer minin' till it played out. He opened a store in Buckskin Joe, over by Canon City, and did all right for a few years. He missed the life over here and wanted to strike it rich, so they moved back in '68 and opened a store at Oro City Number One, where Leadville is now. He's a good man, generous to a fault. He's grubstaked I don't know how many prospectors. He just hates to see the boys go hungry."

"You're talking about Tabor?" Beat asked as he approached and pulled up a chair to join us. "I've heard the story of that family. Augusta's his wife, Maine-born and every inch an honest Yankee trader. While Horace ran the store, she took in boarders and cooked for the miners. The miners loved them for their generosity."

"Why do you call him 'Haw'?" Tilman asked.

"Well, his name is Horace Austin Warner Tabor. He never cared for any of them handles."

Butter continued the story. "Back in April of last year Haw grubstaked a couple of Germans, and a month later their mine, the Little Pittsburgh, hit a bonanza. Folks around the bar at the Double Eagle say he got a dividend of near ten thousand dollars. Old Haw is a-doing right well."

Beat pulled a collapsing telescope from a coat pocket and extended it with practiced ease. He scanned the road to the east, and announced, "Here they come."

The next morning Tilman rose early. Wa had made coffee and set out some of Stab's fry bread and a pot of honey for breakfast. Not seeing the old girl in the kitchen, Tilman guessed she kept to herself when folks were around. As he ate he thought about last night.

Old Wa was a fine cook so Tilman had had no complaints

there. Beat was a genial host, a man with a thousand stories to tell about his life at sea and the exotic-sounding places he's visited. Nevertheless, Tilman felt ill at ease. Tabor was a married man, yet he was being pretty friendly with the two ladies—actresses, they said they were—who came with McRae. It's true they were pretty in the lamplight, but probably looked different in the harsh reality of daylight, without all that paint. As the night wore on, the more they drank, the friendlier they became. Tilman had no idea what the story was with Tabor and his wife, but a man shouldn't do that; it just didn't look right to him. It had been an uncomfortable evening for him, so he made excuses and headed for the blankets.

After his breakfast Tilman walked back to the room and could hear Butter's snoring next door. Amazing. Last night Butter seemed to have an unquenchable thirst for champagne, and McRae had brought more than enough for all of them. Butter'd be sorry today. Tilman decided to go for a ride, and, pulling on an extra shirt to offset the chill in the air, headed for the stables. When he got to the barn he was surprised to find Tabor in there saddling a horse. After exchanging pleasantries Tabor told Tilman he was going to look at some property, and would enjoy the company if Tilman cared to ride along. Thinking it would be a good chance to look around, Tilman agreed.

"You don't approve of me, do you?" Tabor asked as they skirted the lake to look at lots near the Interlaken Hotel.

Tilman laughed. "You get right to the point, don't you?"

"You didn't talk much last night. I sensed your dislike."

"I don't know you well enough to dislike you, Tabor. But since you asked, I don't approve of a married man out womanizing."

"Hate the sin, love the sinner, eh?"

"No, I hate both about equally." Tilman could tell that Tabor didn't expect to hear such hurtful words. "Tabor, don't ask me a question unless you're ready to hear exactly what I'm thinking."

"You don't understand what it's like. Life with Augusta is not easy. I've worked hard to do well, and I think my day has come."

Tilman wondered why Tabor felt he had to explain anything. Surely he was not trying to justify his actions to ease his conscience, or was he?

"Augusta is a good, sensible New England woman, modest and frugal, who's always worked hard for everything we own. I'll be fifty years old next year, and I want to enjoy all the things of the good life. She wants me to lay it aside and be careful."

"She sounds like a sensible person to me." He was making his excuse.

"You don't know what she sounds like," he said, looking hard at Tilman. "Last year I made a bad investment. A man I thought was my friend, 'Chicken' Bill Lovell—you don't know him, do you?—well, he swindled me. I paid ten thousand dollars for the 'Chrysolite,' a mine reputed to have good possibilities. The shaft was twenty feet deep and the ore assayed well, but it turned out that it had been salted with rich ore from another mine—it was worthless. I trusted Bill. When the truth came out, Augusta went on a rampage. I mean to tell you we had a real knock-down, drag-out fight about what she called my wasteful spending. She gave me no peace. I hired some miners to continue sinking the shaft, hoping to strike a vein."

"So there it stands?" Tilman asked.

"No. We've struck a vein of pure silver. It was luck. The assay report said we're looking at nearly a million a year." He smiled. "'Chicken' Bill is the laughingstock of Leadville, now."

"What did Augusta say to that?"

"I haven't told her yet, but I think she suspects my worth

has increased considerably." His voice hardened. "She's gone too far, Wagner. Lately, Maxcy, he's our son, won't have anything to do with me—Augusta has turned him against me because of what she calls my poor investment sense and being such an easy touch for any down and out prospector. She said the way I handle money I'll die in the poor house. Me! A million dollars a year, dying poor! Why, the very idea is ridiculous."

He paused to light a cigar. His hands shook.

"That's how much *she* knows!"

There was desperation in his voice when he continued. Tilman almost felt pity for the man.

"They told me how your son was killed. I sympathize with you for the loss. My son is lost to me almost as surely as yours is to you. You may find and kill the person responsible, but what about me?"

Horace Tabor was a man heading down the wrong path, bent on convincing himself he had a good reason, wanting others to approve of his actions. Tilman found Tabor's comparison of Dan's loss to the situation with his own son to be despicable, and Tilman wanted to be as far away from the man as he could get.

"Adios." Tilman reined his horse back to the trail they'd followed to the Interlaken. Tilman decided to go roust Butter and head back to Mahonville, for he wanted to see Catherine.

Catherine knew that things were fast moving to a conclusion with her and Bill Ward. More and more he seemed to be assuming a proprietary attitude where she was concerned. Bill had invited her to a special dinner at the New Denver Hotel in Mahonville. She feared that Bill was not going to be put off much longer.

"I hear the spring is a good time to begin a new life, Catherine," Bill said, then carefully folded the dark red napkin after a dinner of prime rib, mashed potatoes and rolls and green beans. They were waiting for dessert and once again Catherine noticed that Bill didn't wait well at all. For anyone or anything. The waitress bustled into the room bringing a tray with hot pumpkin pie, apologizing for the delay.

"No trouble, Hilda." Catherine sought to ease the woman's discomfort. "We were just talking," Catherine looked at Bill for confirmation, "weren't we, Bill?"

She watched as he forced himself to relax. "Yes, Hilda. That's fine."

He waited till Hilda went back into the kitchen. The dining room was almost empty as most people had eaten and gone. "Now, where were we, Catherine? Oh, yes. You know how I feel about you. Why do you pretend we are just friends when I want us to be more? I want you to marry me and share my life with me."

Her first thought was, a proposal, here? And immediately she realized there was no mention of James. He always forgot James. That was important. Maybe he didn't mean anything by it, but she noticed.

Bill continued, unaware of her hesitation. "I plan to own most of this town in the next year or two. I have big plans and I need a wife to be by my side." He picked at his pie, as usual, denying himself the enjoyment of such a culinary delight. "You are good looking, smart, and will be an asset in every way."

Catherine was amused. "Bill, you sound like I am another investment you are making. I hear nothing about love, and not being able to live without me, and—"

"Catherine! We are adults. Not two infatuated youngsters." He fidgeted in his seat. "Of course I care for you. Besides," he leaned closer, "you need a man to look after you and your ranch and," he seemed to remember, "and James. He needs a father figure and someone to help him pay for college." There was quiet for a moment. "In fact, he might even want to go to Denver to boarding school for high school. His education would be much more thorough." He sipped his coffee, smug in his assessment of their relationship.

Warning bells went off in Catherine's head. High school—boarding school—no! The kind of relationship he talked about was a business arrangement, not a marriage. "Bill, we shouldn't rush things. We have differences that must be resolved before we can go any further."

Her voice trailed off, her heart did a funny little flip as Tilman stepped through the doorway of the dining room. Something about him spoke of the hard life he had lived, the challenges he had met, and the man he would be again after he found the man who killed his son. And, Catherine thought to herself, after he found peace. Catherine was drawn to Tilman in a way she couldn't explain.

"Evening, Catherine," he smiled warmly. The smile disappeared. "Ward." Tilman stood looking down at the two of them, uninvited, yet secure in his right to be there. Bill, obviously miffed to have his planning session interrupted, growled a muffled greeting, pointedly turning away in his chair and making it obvious he wasn't interested in a conversation with the man standing beside them.

"When did you get back? What brings you to town so late, Tilman?" Catherine suddenly looked alarmed. "James is okay isn't he?" Anxiously, she started to rise, but felt Tilman's strong, calloused hand on her shoulder as he gently guided her back into her seat.

"Got back late this afternoon. James is fine, Catherine. He went to bed just as I left." Tilman's eyes searched the hotel dining room. "I remembered there was something a friend told me to look for in the hotel record books. I was restless so I came in. That is all there is to it." He didn't tell her that James was worried about his mother and Mister Ward. He couldn't tell her that he silently agreed with her son. He just told James that he would come and check on what was happening and now he found himself here, feeling foolish as could be but glad to see Catherine's serene face smiling at him, even though she looked quite confused.

"Records, Tilman? What—"

"Mister Wagner," Ward interrupted, "you can't just go through records like you own the place." Indignant, Bill glowered, obviously upset as he pushed his chair back and stood facing Tilman.

Catherine couldn't help comparing the two of them. Bill appeared polished like a black marble stone, driven by a need to control everything. Tilman looked dusty and rumpled, a genuine forthrightness about him, yet a man also driven by his brand of justice. Catherine shook her head. What an imagination. She also rose. "Well, if you are finished, I think it is time that I go home, Bill." Turning, she nodded. "Tilman." She gracefully started for the door.

Bill had no choice but to throw some money down on the table and follow, knowing that whatever more was going to be said about the future would wait for another day. That Wagner fellow was getting in the way and needed to be stopped before he did any more harm. We'll see about that, Bill thought.

Chapter Eighteen

Tilman was confused. If Catherine was glad he was back she hid it well. She was civil when he returned from Twin Lakes but certainly no more than that. It must be that she had some feelings for Bill Ward. She had as much as said so when she told Tilman about all the things Bill had planned for Mahonville. She'd not ever given Tilman reason to believe she thought of him as anything more than Dan's father, just an acquaintance.

But Tilman had a feeling she was wrong about Bill Ward, that Ward's bid for respectability was only a cover. Bat Masterson was certain about Ward, and for sure Butter knew about him. Smiley made no bones about who and what he was, and he seemed to be satisfied with his current lot. Tilman couldn't see how Smiley was involved in anything relating to Dan.

Bill Ward was interested in Catherine. That's true. And Dan took a room at Catherine's boardinghouse, also true, which fed the town's gossip mill, another truth. Who was Bill Ward and where did he come from? Tilman had learned that Bill Ward was a man of two personalities, one a seedy gambling parlor owner and saloonkeeper with a stable of women upstairs, the other a respectable banker and civic leader who attended church and gave generously of his money, even helped down and out prospectors. The truth about *what* Bill was depended on who was doing the talking. Tilman learned long ago that more than one slick citizen in this world bought his respectability and high social standing with money from ill-gotten gains, and not only there in Mahonville. That story was as old as mankind. There was another possibility. Could it boil down to a quarrel over a woman if Ward thought that Dan was getting in his way and he needed Catherine to fit his idea of respectability? Tilman had little to go on but his own suspicions. He needed to know more.

In town Tilman stopped by Aunt Mae's Restaurant across from the Silver King. He'd got to know Mae and her husband Dolph Schulenberg, who ran the place. They'd no kids of their own, but had taken in some family extras to raise. Miss Alma, Mae's oldest niece, was waitress today. She was about eighteen, and the boys called her Slats because she was tall and on the skinny side. She was hunting for a decent man to marry, and she'd set her sights on Tilman as worth a try, even if he was a bit old for her. Alma brought out something she called "oily cakes," raised doughnuts sprinkled with sugar and cinnamon. She made them herself hoping Tilman would come in, or so she said. She was a talker and all but hovered over Tilman, touching his shoulder with her hand, smiling and cutting her eyes at him, and then took a seat across the table from Tilman to watch him eat.

That grocery clerk Tilman had seen the day he had a run-in with Shorty sat across the room taking it all in. Poor moonstruck boy, hung around whenever he could hoping she'd notice him, and Tilman knew he'd just love for her to bring him a doughnut and sit by him. The boy saw Miss Alma reach across the table to touch Tilman's hand, her fingers lingering on his. Tilman suddenly remembered how he felt when he saw Catherine touching Bill Ward's arm the day of the church meeting. Tilman gently withdrew his hand and told Miss Alma she had an admirer sitting at a table across the room. She glanced at the boy, and then dismissed him with a carefully practiced toss of her suspiciously bright yellow hair. Tilman had heard of women putting lemon juice on their hair to brighten it, and he thought Miss Alma might be overdoing it a bit.

"Oh, him. That's just Jackie. He's still a boy." She beamed at Tilman. "Not like you."

This could be trouble. Lucky for Tilman, Miss Alma got busy with the early supper crowd, so he decided to look into Ward's business at the Silver King Saloon, Mahonville's newest. Crossing the street, Tilman found Sheriff and Butter at a table near the bar, where he joined them.

Butter complained, "My stummick ain't got over all the champagne I drunk when we were staying at Beat's hotel up at Twin Lakes, so I'm a-drinking coffee from now on."

"Does that mean you've taken the pledge nevermore to consort with old John Barleycorn?" Tilman teased.

"For today, anyhow."

"I ain't been in here before. Look at them nekkid women in the pictures!" Sheriff said pointing at the series of colorful paintings over the polished mahogany bar, showing reclining women wearing nothing more than strategically placed veils.

They agreed that somebody had spent a lot of money to set up this place. To the left of the front entrance was a closed door with a sign that read OFFICE. The imported, hand-carved mahogany bar, still free of the imprint from the many spurs that would be left by cowhands, cuts and gouges from miners and other men, ran the length of the left side of the room. At the back was a raised stage with foot lights and scenes of snow-capped mountains brightly painted on a canvas backdrop. To the side was a lower platform for the "orchestra," which at present was three men in blackface wearing red jackets with white piping, white duck trousers, white canvas shoes, and straw boaters. The instruments seemed limited to a piano, banjo and trumpet, but what they lacked in number they made up for in noise, for they all but drowned out conversation in the room. To the right were stairs leading to a balcony of curtained "birdcages," where a man could watch the show in private with whatever hostess he fancied. There were other rooms up there too.

Even though it was early in the evening, the place was packed with humanity—swells, dandies, gamblers, miners, teamsters, lumber men, serving girls, and buy-me-a-drink girls working the crowd. There was much coming and going of people up the stairs to the birdcages and rooms.

"Gambling games here beat anything I ever saw," Sheriff said. "They got roulette, poker, blackjack, and 'buck the tiger.' Why, you name it and it's here!"

"I'd just as soon sit outside on a sunny day and play Texas Forty-two," Butter snorted. "Dominoes is my game."

The orchestra took a break, and a once-distinguished looking man, now merely a travesty of respectability wearing a stained long black cape, took the stage. With broadly sweeping dramatic movements, no doubt often practiced before a mirror, he began to recite Shakespeare in a stentorian voice. For a moment the man seemed to forget where he was and in his mind imagined himself young again and back on the boards. The culturally starved crowd, so far removed from times past and different worlds, quieted down to listen respectfully.

Tilman took the time to study the men around them, looking for Bill Ward. There was a lot of hard drinking and gambling going on, mostly by men hoping to get rich gambling if not by mining. The more they drank, the more desperately they gambled. A sober observer would easily see that the only ones getting rich were the men running the games after, of course, passing a cut to the saloon owners. It was a grim circle of lost hope with no way to go but further and further down.

A familiar face at the bar attracted Tilman's eyes. It was the man from the stage station at South Arkansas, the Mexican. "Butter, do you see that fellow?"

"That's the son of a gun from. . . ."

"That's Blas Mendoza, the Silver City, New Mexico bounty hunter," Sheriff said, turning his upper body and his head around in order to see out of his good eye. "I knew he was in town."

Blas caught Tilman's eye and nodded. He picked up his drink and came to the table, hooked the toe of his boot under the leg of a chair to pull it out, and then sat with them. It was a neat way of keeping his gun-hand free while he carried his drink. This was the second time Tilman had seen him up close, but this time he looked more carefully at the dark-complexioned man, contrasting white teeth showing as he smiled, a buff-colored sombrero, stitched with shiny turquoise threads, hanging down his back by the stampede string, his shiny black hair carefully combed. His thin mustache was waxed, and a small wedge of beard grew below the center of his lower lip. He must be nearing thirty years old, vain about his looks, Tilman thought, a real cock-of-the walk.

"We've met before, *es verdade, senor?*"

"*Si, verdade.* You are not the kind of man one soon forgets."

"That day I saw you at the *salida,* the place to leave the valley, you were on the stage and I was looking for a *gringo* man, big, like you. I thought maybe you were that man, *senor.* I had to be sure, but I did not mean to frighten you," he laughed, his flashing teeth white as the snow against his tanned face.

"*Amigo,* I was just being mighty careful that day."

"*Si, cuidado.* I, too, was being careful, as you say. *Muy bien*, we must not fight each other. Now it is time we should be *compadres.* You search for a man, your son's killer. A man must avenge his family, an eye for an eye, *senor.* It is a man's way. This I know. I search for a man, he calls himself Johnny Russell, from the *malpais* north of the border with old Mexico. We must take care, you and I, we do not get in each other's way.

"This man I seek," he continued, "Russell, his *madre* runs a, *como usted dice?* Uh, a house of bad women, in Silver City. His *madre*, she owns two such houses in Tucson and yet another in Nogales, so she has plenty dollars. This *Juanito* is a very bad man; he loves to eat the worm in *mescal*, and some say he is fond of the pipe smoked by *los Chinos*. Once when he had been drunk for three days, he got in a fight with *su hermano*, his brother. When the brother pulled a big knife and began cutting *Juanito*, he would not stop, so *Juanito* got his mother's *pistola*, a small silver one, and killed his brother right there in the front yard of his mother's house. *La senora* Russell put up a thousand-dollar bounty. 'Dead or alive,' she said. For her own *hijo*, imagine!

"You know, I was ver' close to finding him in a mining town near Durango, not the one in Mexico but the one west of here, on the River of Souls. I think he got away last year about the same time somebody robbed one of the mines. I think Russell was this robber, and it is possible he is now in this town, Mahonville."

"Why do you think he's here?" Tilman asked.

"A dying man told me this," said Blas.

"Who? Why would anyone tell you anything like that?"

"He was one of the guards at the mine who helped with the robbery," Blas said, pulling a short but wicked looking knife from his boot top and stabbing it into the center of the table, "so I asked him very politely to talk to me. He talked for *mi pequeno cuchillo*." He smiled coldly as he retrieved his knife and replaced it in his boot-top sheath. "But then, *pobrecito*, he died. Too bad, eh?"

At the thought of how Blas got his information, Tilman felt a chill; was he dealing with the devil here? That mustache and beard—he even *looked* like the devil! What kind of man would do such a thing? Tilman thought Blas was evil incarnate the first time he saw him, now he was sure of it.

Butter cleared his throat as he slowly withdrew his hands from the table, the whites of his eyes showing all around. Sheriff had a slight, surprised smile on his face, not sure if he had heard correctly that Blas had admitted to a cold-blooded murder.

"I don't know for sure, but so far I have not seen this man," an unconcerned Blas continued. "He must have changed the way he looks, but he cannot change what he is. I will find him, and with the money I will go back to Saltillo, marry and become a rancher, *mas gordo y mas rico que siempre antes*, fatter and richer than ever before. I will have many children, and I will have a new life."

As he spoke, a faraway look came into his eyes, and for a brief moment he didn't look quite so fierce and deadly. But the look quickly disappeared.

"A drink to our success, *senores*, and my new *rancho*." He called one of the server girls over. "*Querida senorita*, bring us *tequila*, limes, and salt; my new friends and I will drink to our health and success."

Out came the knife again, only this time not so forcefully, to slice the limes.

Tilman sat up straighter in his chair. He couldn't let on to Blas that his confession was bothersome, to say the least.

"Sure, let's have a shot." Was Tilman really going to deal with the devil to get what he wanted? Had he come to that? There was no way out of this without appearing weak, and Blas was the kind of man who would see weakness and use it against a man to get what he wanted.

While Blas poured a shot, Tilman took a dripping wedge of lime between the thumb and forefinger of his right hand, salted the web of skin behind them, raised the glass with *"Salud"* and licked the salt, downed the fiery tequila, and then bit the lime savoring the tart goodness of the juice.

Tilman! You know what drink does to you!

"Hush!" Her again.

"*Perdon, senor*, what did you say?" Blas's eyes quickly

became guarded, reminding Tilman of snake eyes which suddenly become hooded against danger.

"*Amigo*, if I told you who I was talking to you would really think I was *loco*!" Tilman shook his head, once again amazed at how Sarah never let him alone for a minute. Even for a little *tequila*—or was it because of the man he drank it with?

At the bar near their table a fancied-up dude pulled a sack of Bull Durham and papers from his green-checked coat and tried to roll a smoke one-handed, to the great fascination of three nearby drunks. He succeeded only in sprinkling tobacco on the bar. The dude gave up and ordered a glass of Port wine and pulled a cigar from his coat. The drunks started to laugh and make fun of him, and then it turned ugly.

"Hey, Mister Remittance Man, did you leave home sudden-like because somebody's daughter turned up a family way?"

"Are you one of the royal highnesses just come to see how us poor old colonials are getting along?"

"We'd be glad to show you how we're doing."

"Come on boys, I know where there's tar and feathers. Let's us show him the town from the back of a rail."

Having none of that, the dude faced the three and with a lightning draw produced a gun from the shoulder holster under his jacket. All at once, the drunks sobered up and the room became still.

"I'd rather show *you* the gates of hell," he said quietly.

Tilman listened attentively, for the dude spoke with an English accent.

Sheriff leaned near and whispered urgently, "That feller came to town about the time Dan was killed, I remember now because he was a different sort an' he kept his hoss at the livery a month or so but I ain't seed him since. Kind of a standout for he weren't like any of them others."

"Come, gentlemen. Let's not be shy," the dude taunted, "who shall be the first?"

He was mighty calm for a man facing three hardcase miners. He didn't look like he'd have the backbone for it—a slightly built sandy-haired young man; pale, with soft-looking hands, maybe a gambler. The cut of his coat indicated a man who was used to money; brushed velvet patches protected his elbows and the herringbone tweed bespoke a life of privilege in upper class England. When he opened his mouth, Tilman no longer had any doubts. His accent was pure and from the best schools of Europe, far from the gutters and slums. Interesting! Why was such a man here?

Two brawny house toughs elbowed their way though the curious, hushed crowd behind the miners and the larger of the two deftly laid a slap behind the ear of a miner, who dropped like a pole-axed steer.

"Pick him up and get out," one of the toughs growled, slipping brass knuckles over his right hand in case the other two didn't get the message. "Don't bother coming back."

The two now quiet and subdued miners dragged their unconscious friend out of the bar. The on-stage oratory had ended with the ruckus, but now that the situation was under control, the orchestra began merrily tootling away.

The dude dropped the pistol back into its holster. After he'd adjusted his coat, he stared into the mirror behind the bar, lighting the cigar. Calmly he sipped the wine he'd ordered. Tilman studied the man's reflected image in the mirror as their eyes met. The dude looked away.

Sheriff started in where he'd left off. "I recollect he wore leather bottom riding britches and high-topped boots polished ever so nice, an' silver spurs, big Spanish rowels you don't see this far north, with jinglebobs so's you'd hear him comin' down the boardwalk. A real swell."

"Sheriff, see what else you can find out about him." Tilman guessed that, as the drunks had said, he probably was a remittance man sent out west because he embarrassed the family. Tilman had seen several of them in other times and other places.

Just then Ward stepped out of the saloon's business office and spoke quietly to the Englishman, "Mister Johnson, I'd like a word with you."

Johnson walked across the room to enter the office and as he passed, Tilman heard the sound of small bells. James had said one of the men who threatened Dan made a sound like bells. Tilman looked and sure enough, the man wore spurs—fancy silver Mexican spurs with two-inch rowels and jingle-bobs to make the sound of small bells!

One of the serving girls followed Johnson into the office with a bottle of mescal and a couple of glasses on a tray. When she came out and closed the door behind her, Tilman looked around and saw that Blas, moving as soundlessly as a stalking panther, had gone. A chill passed over Tilman although there was no breeze in the saloon.

Chapter Nineteen

Conversation resumed around the room, leaving Tilman, Butter and Sheriff deep in thought. Tilman realized that he had to begin to piece the parts of the puzzle together.

"Boys, let's take a look at what we know," he said to Butter and Sheriff, "but first a question. This Ward, when did he come to town?"

"'Bout this time a year ago, ain't that right, Butter?" Sheriff answered.

"Yeah, it was. And come to think of it, Shorty Bain came right after Ward. I remember it because that's about the time he beat up a crib girl real bad." Butter nodded in assent. "Right off Ward set hisself up as a law an' order man with the vigilance committee, and I heard he bought half interest in the Miner's and Rancher's Bank."

"Where did he come from?" Tilman asked.

"Folks around here generally don't ask if a man don't volunteer such as that," Butter offered. "It ain't polite an' it ain't healthy."

Sheriff took up the story. "About that same time somebody talked old Smiley into splitting the town down the middle with Ward. Then Ward started building this here saloon."

"Smiley was laid up for quite a while after that." Butter added, "Folks said he was beat near to death."

"Did Ward do it?"

"If he did, you couldn't tell lookin' at his hands," Sheriff said. "He probably hired somebody from out of town to do it."

"So, Ward comes in from who-knows-where, with enough of a bankroll to start right off with a respectable business," Tilman said. "He's friendly, grubstakes prospectors, and makes a show of helping the poor and being all for law and order. Nobody knows his background. He's just a very civic-minded, church-going gent. Not bad for a stranger, I'd say."

Butter and Sheriff listened carefully.

"Most folks get so busy with their own lives they don't notice he's got something else going on the shady side," Tilman added. "They see only what he wants them to see. What does he not want us to know?" Silence became the fourth partner at the table.

"Why would he be interested in the stage timetables?" Butter asked. "Remember what James said? He told us that Ward asked Dan about stage arrival times." A worried look came over his face. "I'm the company's only driver for the treasure wagon. We don't stick to no reg'lar schedule."

"Keep going."

"The schedule is a secret, Tilman, known only by a few people."

"Would Dan, as stationmaster, have been one of the few?"

"He knew," Butter said. "I start the run with a pickup from Granite where most of the gold dust and bullion is loaded, then come down to Mahonville for smaller amounts. After that I cross Trout Creek Pass to the rail terminal at the town of Como, for shipment by rail to Denver."

"It seems to me that right now Ward could be in the perfect place at the perfect time to pull a high-grade ore and bullion job here in Mahonville." Tilman leaned across the table to speak quietly. "Skinny Morris told me about a big thing over near Durango last year. Preacher Fry can back me up because he was there. Somebody made off with a lot of gold. Blas was there too, but lost track of the man he was looking for about the same time." Things were falling into place for a pretty good circumstantial case against Ward.

"Let me see if I got that straight," Butter said. "You think Ward is the man who goes from boomtown to boomtown stealing ore and bullion. And, he might be the one Blas is looking for."

"Right, and Shorty may be the actual shooter," Tilman suggested, "the one who does Ward's dirty work. He killed Dan. What do you think?"

"Where does Johnson fit in?" Butter asked. "James said he was with Ward that day, y'know, the sound of bells when he walks?"

"That there's another possibility," Sheriff said. "We know Ward wanted Dan to give him the schedule and Dan refused. That means Ward, if he planned to rob the treasure wagon, tipped his hand. He could have hired Johnson to kill Dan to keep him quiet, ain't that right?"

"Well, yes, but," Tilman said, "Johnson doesn't seem like a man who'd use a Sharps Big Fifty. I'd say that's more Shorty's style."

"But I ain't heard nobody talking about Shorty out target shooting at Five Elks," Butter said, "and them fellers I seen that day didn't none of them look like Shorty, so my money's on Johnson." Butter's skeptical look told Tilman what he thought of that suggestion about Shorty. No one mentioned Blas. A killer he might be, but he didn't fit this wanted poster.

As Tilman spoke, Johnson came out of Ward's office plainly irritated at whatever had occurred inside, and left the saloon. Had Johnson been the one to threaten Dan? Ward now stood in the door to his office, looked to the bar, this time where Shorty Bain was standing and called him in next. The realization that Ward, Johnson and Shorty were all working together on something suddenly seemed unmistakable.

It wasn't long before Shorty came out of the office, went back to the bar and began drinking and hugging on one of the girls—Lou, he called her—while whispering in her ear.

Stepping up to the bar and getting a deck of cards from the barkeep, Tilman tried to get a closer look at Shorty. He quickly learned that Shorty was feeling his drinks because he was loudly bragging to the woman how he'd soon be rich, and anybody got in the way, well him and the boss would take care of him—like with that Texas boy. He may be mean, Tilman observed, but the way he talked, Shorty must be all muscle and little brain. Suddenly Shorty grabbed the woman by the arm and started to pull her toward the stairs.

Lou didn't want to go and resisted. "Shorty, I warned you last time that unless you took a bath and sobered up I would not go with you." Her expression reflected memories of other times and none of them appeared to be pleasant.

Shorty brutally grabbed her arm and threw her toward the stairs, cursing viciously. "Don't you go actin' the swell with me," he said. "You're nobody but a saloon girl."

That was enough! A vision of Shorty grabbing Catherine sparked Tilman's anger. Deciding Shorty needed to be taken down a notch, Tilman swung hard and laid his fist to the side of Shorty's head sending him crashing to the floor. The girl, after a grateful glance in Tilman's direction, ran from the room. Taking a handful of soiled shirt front Tilman lifted a dazed, disgustingly smelly and semiconscious Shorty up and backed him against the wall. Holding him up there with his right hand, Shorty's feet dangling, Tilman stripped Shorty's gunbelt off and let it drop to the floor. Tilman knew the drunk would probably have a sore head tomorrow.

"Stand easy, boys," Butter said to the house toughs. "This here's private."

Tilman dragged Shorty to the door and across the boardwalk. He threw him out into the dark street, spooking a couple of horses tied at the rail, and there Shorty fell in an unmoving, sour-smelling heap. The cool night air would help sober him up. Shorty had no right to treat that girl, or any girl, the way he did. Trying to make a living and get by, same as anyone, she lived the best way she knew. Tilman wondered what it was about some men who couldn't feel like a man unless they slapped a woman around. Or, for that matter, like that little drunk in the saloon at Granite; anybody they thought they could bully and not have a fight on their hands. Mahonville reminded him of turning over rocks in a dark, damp place. One never knew what kind of bug or slimy thing was under there to scurry away from the light.

"Shorty hates better than anyone in the county," Sheriff said, "so watch out."

"Gents." One of the saloon toughs nodded toward the front door, and said, "Come back another night."

Tilman had seen more than enough for one night. But, yes, he thought, he'd come back another day to see what else he could learn about Ward.

Chapter Twenty

As before, Tilman found sleep an elusive stranger. That was getting to be a bad habit. Daybreak the next morning found him sitting in Aunt Mae's Restaurant with a cup of coffee, watching the Silver King across the street. Miss Alma must have worked late the night before, because the cook was waiting tables. Just as well, for Tilman was not up to being fawned over and touched and smiled at today. He was on edge. His mind was troubled but he felt he was close to finding the man who killed Dan.

Shorty came out of the saloon, walked to the edge of the boardwalk and threw up in the street. He was nauseous after last night's ruckus with Tilman. That chunk on the head from Tilman's fist left Shorty with a mean headache, and though he'd started his day with some "hair of the dog" . . . the drink didn't help. Shorty was not far from having what folks called the shakes, the *delirium tremens* because he drank so much liquor. Nobody would say it to his face, but Shorty depended on alcohol to shore up his self-respect.

While Tilman watched Shorty, Miss Alma stepped into the room from the kitchen with a fresh pot of coffee, going from table to table, calling out a cheery "Good morning" to each early customer. She reserved her most radiant smile for, who else? Tilman.

"More coffee, dear?" Her fingers trailed along his neck.

Dear? This has got to stop. A man twice her age! Where is that boy Jackie?

In the midst of Miss Alma's flirtatious salutation, Tilman spotted Shorty once again. Shorty continued his miserable morning ritual as he washed his face in a horse trough, dried it on his coat sleeve, and mounted up to ride out of town. Tilman dropped two bits on the table for the breakfast, quickly muttered excuses to a stunned Miss Alma, and departed, followed by the beginnings of a loud and heartfelt set of sniffles. *Oh, brother. What will I have to do to get out of this one?*

As Tilman made his way to the door, one man sitting near a window smiled at Miss Alma, winked and called out, "Hey, dear." He pronounced 'dear' in a quavering falsetto. "How 'bout some of that coffee over here, Slats?"

She blushed, quickly forgot her tears and hurried over to his table.

Tilman went out and climbed aboard his paloose. Keeping well back, he followed Shorty out of town and up the road towards Cottonwood Pass. As he neared Catherine's place, Tilman saw her out front. Recognizing the horse, she waved, just as she'd wave to any friend or acquaintance.

Tilman was sure there was no other meaning in it. Did he want to be more than just friends with Catherine Stone? Was he finally ready to deal with a real live woman instead of memories of Sarah? Questions he wasn't quite ready to answer. He had to solve Dan's murder before he could do anything else.

Turning Needles aside he headed over to Catherine. He told himself he owed it to her to let her know the direction he was heading since he might have to make camp and didn't want her worrying about where he was. At least that's how he justified what he was about to do. He knew it was foolish even to assume she might care so he hesitated, then started to turn back, for Shorty was moving out of sight.

"Tilman. Where are you going?" Catherine appeared alongside Needles, looking up. He must have been moving towards her without being aware.

"Catherine." He swung down from the saddle and stood by her side. She wasn't that tall, yet she was so calm and self-assured that he'd forgotten she barely came to his shoulder. "I'm heading up into the hills. I'm following Shorty. I think he might be up to something. If I'm not back for supper, don't worry." Tilman felt the sudden need to touch her face, maybe for reassurance that all was well, but his hand didn't move. He turned and got back on the horse. She stood there watching, curious, wondering why Tilman suddenly decided to tell her where he was heading, since he didn't usually.

She nodded a wordless assent, then, "Be careful, Tilman. That is all I ask."

Tilman rode off quickly, hoping that Shorty's excesses the night before had kept him slowed down.

Did Catherine see that he had his gun belt on? What would she think? He was so distracted by thoughts about the widow he failed to clear his back trail while still out on the open plain. As the trail entered the narrow canyon, the walls were so steep and the wagon road so narrow it was impossible to circle to clear his back trail. He felt uneasy about being so closed in, but had to stay near Shorty. Climbing higher, he shivered in the cool morning air, and saw ice formed on the edges of the creek. Needles was breathing harder, his breath making puffs of steam going up the steep trail. Coming from such hot, humid climates, between growing up in North Carolina and now living in south Texas, Tilman wondered how the men working here were able to survive the bone-chilling cold that Colorado winters were supposed to be all about. It might be beautiful, but it was also dangerous and he had heard many a man had lost his life to the elements. Once the snows began, lives could hang in the balance of a hand too stiff or feet too frozen to move in time when avalanches came tumbling down. At that time, nature clearly held the upper hand and the men employed building and working the railroad were truly at the mercy of Mother Nature. Mining people could have their cold and grim existence. Tilman liked open fields and the low, rolling Texas hill country.

After several uncomfortable minutes of glancing over his shoulder Tilman was able to climb to a perilously steep ridge that pushed out into the narrow canyon and see his back trail. Tilman didn't want to lose Shorty, and seeing no one following behind, he hurried on. Soon the valley became wider, more open as Shorty passed through a small settlement of rough-cut pine slab and log shanties and crude dugouts at what had to be the place where South Cottonwood Creek joined Cottonwood Creek. If that was right, then this was Harvard City, a little town left over from a gold boom and bust four or five years ago. A steam engine at the sawmill stood silent on a flat across the creek, waiting for the first shift of workers. A tow-headed boy was laying cut wood in the firebox under the boiler, getting ready to make steam. Many of the lumbermen in this area were Scandinavian and even from afar, Tilman reckoned by the young boy's snow-white hair that he was from that stock. Stacks of raw spruce logs had been snaked down from the hills for sawing. A mule brayed. The smell of wood smoke came from cooking fires in the cabins, and somebody was frying bacon. A woman's complaining voice broke the still morning air and a man coughed and spat. Tilman took care to make no noise. Watching Shorty, Tilman stuck cold hands under his armpits to warm them. Cold-stiffened fingers can get a man killed if he has to use a gun sudden-like. A bearded old man dressed in dirty, worn bib overalls and high rubber boots sat on a rough-cut bench in front of a store in the cool shadows waiting for the morning sun to warm him. The man spoke to Shorty, who ignored him. Then, as Shorty turned up a side trail, Tilman circled around the settlement to get behind him again. A cool wind began to blow down from the heights of the pass, sighing through the tall spruce trees. Good. Tilman was downwind, and that would mask any sound he might make. The trees thinned out, and about a hundred yards off he saw Shorty unsaddle his horse and turn him loose in a small pole corral, then throw the saddle onto the top fence rail.

Tilman shucked his boots and pulled on his moccasins, and used what cover there was in the rough ground to provide concealment. He Indianed up carefully to get a little closer. He saw a mine cut into one side of the mountain maybe twenty feet above the bottom of the steep-sided u-shaped valley. Yellowish dirt and rock dug from the mine had been dumped to form a broad apron in front of the portal. Shorty stood by the fence, fished a bottle out of his saddlebags, and turned it up and took a long swallow, gagged, spit, and took another. He was drinking some of the local homemade rotgut. A man Tilman once knew in Tascosa, up in the Texas panhandle, used to make what he called "Injun Whiskey." He'd mix up a concoction of cut plug tobacco, a dozen or so dried red chile peppers and then toss in a handful of gunpowder. He'd add a little water, boil the mess and sort of strain it, and then mix it with some cheap whiskey to stretch it. He said the tobacco gave his whiskey a nice musty taste, and the peppers gave it a bite. He never did say what the gunpowder did. Folks said that if you fed a dog gunpowder it would make him mean, so why not a man too? That was probably one of the reasons there were so many mean drunks around Tascosa. If that was what Shorty was drinking now, that would explain his short temper!

An old dugout near the mine had fallen in, but out front, looking very out of place amid rusting cans and trash, stood a single white kitchen chair that had seen better days. Shorty disappeared inside the mine portal. The surrounding mountains were sparsely covered with pines and aspens, mostly deformed or diseased culls, because most of the good timber had been cut and sent to sawmills to provide building planks, mine shoring, and now railroad ties for the coming railroad. Back in North Carolina Tilman's neighbor, "Seef" Miller, had clear-cut a quarter section and ruined what had been a beautiful forest of tall pines along the Yadkin River. Civilization brought conveniences and made life easier in many ways, but it also took from the earth in ways that were not often pleasant to see. Across the hillside among the remaining trees several large granite boulders had been dropped in odd places here and there by retreating glaciers.

In the quiet, a large bull elk appeared near a fast-growing grove of young aspens, and began to bite off chunks of bark. Elk were the cause of the black scars often found on aspen trunks. The animal's coat blended in with the denuded trees. His rack of antlers would make any hunter the envy of his friends. Tilman waited patiently, but about an hour later, clouds began rolling in and changing the deep blue sky to gray; the wind picked up, and the temperature began falling. Shorty came out, looked at the sky, hit that bottle once again, then saddled his bronc and mounted up. Tilman watched as he rode back down the mountain the way he'd come. When Shorty was out of sight Tilman got his horse and rode up to look at the tunnel. Up close it was obvious the mine hadn't been worked in a while. Several short-handled jackhammers and dulled rusted hand-drilling steels lay at the entrance near a pile of empty, broken Giant powder boxes and a mostly used up roll of fuse. A worn-out shovel—folks here called them "muck sticks"—leaned against a wall. A wooden box of blasting caps sat in a cubby cut into the rock. As he searched for information about Dan, Tilman had learned what it was like inside one of the mines; men sweating and cursing the heat under flickering candlelight, swinging heavy jackhammers to strike the drill—"single-jacking" was what they called hand drilling by one man. If one trusting miner held the drill while his pard swung a jackhammer, they called it "double-jacking." A missed swing could cost a man his hand. That was a hard way to earn a living, and not one for Tilman. Progress had to be slow unless they could afford to use giant powder to blow down or "pull" several feet off the face of a tunnel at a time, then muck out the rubble.

Inside, the narrow main drift was only about six feet high, barely three wide, and went straight into the mountain for about a hundred feet. The shoring timbers seemed sturdy enough. There were two lateral drifts angling off the main tunnel where they'd followed a promising mineral vein. As Tilman looked in, a draft of air blew against his cheeks. Somebody had cut a ventilation shaft, so it must have been a going concern, at least at one time. Now, for a plainsman, used to seeing lots of sky and wide-open prairie, Tilman didn't care for such closed-in places under the ground. He was not comfortable going in that dark place, but Tilman had to see what this was all about. Near the entrance lay a box with a couple of candle stubs, and several spiked candleholders for sticking into shoring timber while a man worked in the mine. There was one oil lamp with a broken globe that Tilman picked up and shook only to find the reservoir empty. He lit two candles and started looking around, but the rising wind blew them out. He looked around some more and found a bucket with about a one-inch hole cut in one side near the bottom. Oddly, there was candle wax around the hole. Then it dawned on Tilman that some inventive miner had made a hood for his candle to both protect it from the wind and reflect the light to where he worked, kind of a makeshift bull's-eye lantern, so Tilman put it to use.

The first drift turned left, and carrying the light in there Tilman found ore bags, forty of them, each filled with chunks of rock and lined up against one side of the drift.

Tilman had learned enough about mining that he could safely say these might contain mineral ore. What he couldn't understand was why anyone would leave it unguarded if it had any value? Shorty was involved, so it must somehow be related to Ward. Tilman needed to get to his horse to bring in the saddlebags to collect some specimens. These he'd take for analysis at one of the town's assay offices. As he neared the portal he heard the wind outside blowing strongly down the valley, so he knew he ought to hurry if he intended to get back down the mountain to the warmth of Catherine's kitchen. The mountains were no place for Tilman during a storm. By hurrying, he got careless. It was a stupid thing to do.

Chapter Twenty-one

Suddenly, splinters burned his neck as a shot slammed into a rock by Tilman's head when he stepped out of the tunnel. The bullet ricocheted downward to bury itself in the dirt. Tilman heard the heavy boom of the shot echo across the mountains as he hit the ground rolling and crawled to cover. *Close!* His eyes wide, senses alert, keenly aware of even the smallest movement and sound, Tilman searched the hills to find the man trying to kill him. Where did the shot come from? Did Shorty circle around and get the drop? If he did he's smarter than Tilman figured. The wind was howling now, masking any sound the shooter might have made. No one was visible outside. Tilman looked up at the bullet strike on the rock, then dug a piece of the ugly, flattened lead slug out of the dirt and marveled at the ragged edges. A ricochet tears a man badly because of those edges. So, what's the difference between a ragged hole and a smooth hole when you get shot? You're still shot. The same kind of marks could be found on those dark gray boulders by Devil's Den south of Gettysburg, and Tilman remembered how a sergeant showed him to look for the angle of the bullet path in order to find where Yankee sharpshooters hid. With a sudden chill Tilman realized that there was a sharpshooter out there and it may be the man who killed Dan! Could that drunk, Shorty, be the one who killed Dan, and now have Tilman under his gun? Could he have been so wrong about a drunk? That drunk may be about to kill Tilman.

Being stalked by a sharpshooter is a quick way to be dead, especially if he knows his business. The advantage was all his, since Tilman was stupid enough to let the shooter catch him under his gun, not knowing the layout of the land here, not even expecting to be hunted like this. Tilman was angry with himself because he gave Shorty such a perfect chance. Tilman ought to have known better! Now he had to get out of there, turn the tables, find Shorty and kill him, but how? Lucky for Tilman that Shorty had been drinking so he must have misjudged the wind. He must have rushed his shot. Maybe he was cold too, and in a hurry. His bad judgment worked in Tilman's favor. Now they were even for each had made a stupid mistake. For either, the next one could be fatal.

Tilman had hunted men in Santa Elena Canyon in the Big Bend country, so he knew that in a narrow valley the wind force was always changing and could come from several directions within a distance of a few hundred yards. He was lucky that storm was coming in. A lucky coincidence. He studied the possible angle of the shot and noticed his horse's ears were up, so Tilman looked where he looked. Tilman moved a bit, looked up and another shot zipped past his head. But this time Tilman saw the muzzle flash and a puff of smoke where the shot came from, up the hill across the valley, about two hundred yards away. Too far to risk exposing himself for a pistol shot. Snow fell, swirling on the wind, and the air grew colder. The sky darkened, and the wind blew even harder, moaning now. Tilman crawled through low scrub brush on his belly near Needles, watching for movement across the valley, speaking softly so as to reassure the paloose. The animal was not used to seeing anybody approach him in a low crawl, and Tilman took care not to spook the horse.

Shivering in the cold, Tilman waited. How long? Thirty minutes? He didn't want to rush it, for if the shooter could see Tilman he'd have hit him by now. Was anybody still up there? Whoever he was, the man was taking one shot at a time—not a repeater like a Henry or Winchester—a Sharps? Tilman's horse was no longer interested in watching, and had turned to push his nose through the ground-cover looking for something to eat. Now! Tilman jumped up and ran the few feet and grabbed his Winchester off the saddle, slapped the horse to send him out of the way. Again Tilman hit the ground rolling as another booming shot spattered dirt around him. Fixing his eyes on the spot where he'd seen the muzzle flash Tilman levered three quick .44-40 rounds at it, the sharp crack of his shots torn away by the wind. There! A flurry of activity in the brush where he'd fired, so Tilman burned two more quick shots at the movement.

"How d'you like that, Shorty?" Tilman shouted above the wind. "Close enough for you?"

Silence, but for the wind.

"C'mon Shorty," he taunted, "come and get me!"

He waited. Nothing.

"Hey, Shorty! Don't you want to come down here and slap me around like you do your women?" Tilman was sure that would get a rise out of Shorty, but he was wrong again. He thought about using a searching fire in the area where he'd seen the movement, but decided that since he had no ammunition reserve, only the ten shots remaining in the rifle, he'd better wait.

The storm built in fury; the snow fell so thickly Tilman could barely see. Cold! How long had he lain among the rocks? An hour? Snow gathered, sifted down the collar of his shirt, and wet it where snow melted from his body heat.

Stiff with cold, shivering, tense from almost being killed, Tilman made his way back into the mine.

Once inside, he collected some of the broken boxes, and crawled back under the ventilation shaft to build a fire, fingers numb, feet like blocks of ice. Tilman used some straw packing, wood splinters for kindling, and quickly got a small fire going. He had no idea what time it was, or how long he'd traded shots with that sharpshooter. Tilman cursed himself for getting caught like a greenhorn, and added fuel to the fire to hold back a penetrating, painful cold. When he'd finally warmed his hands and feet, he rustled up an enameled tin wash pan with a hole in one end, and used that to melt some snow and get a drink of water.

He sat on a box, hands shaking, and added wood to the fire. He hunched over that small fire, listening to the wind howl. It was not just the cold making Tilman's hands shake. After every gunfight he was ever in, that happened. Nerves letting go, letting down as his blood, heated with excitement, cooled. Tilman knew what Pastor Fry meant when he talked about needing excitement. But this hole in the ground almost became a grave. He found himself praying to live long enough to finish this job. Carefully he picked more rock fragments out of his neck, cursed even more for getting trapped. He had never been this cold, and every time the fire burned down, he shivered worse than before. Somebody wanted him dead. Get out now while he still could? Was he losing his nerve like Bat? Doubt came in the night, an uncomfortable presence sharing his cramped resting place. Tilman had never quit before and he didn't intend to now. Not while he still had a job to do.

He slept—minutes? Dreams of Sarah filled the dark and she still appeared angry with him for wanting vengeance. The cold woke Tilman, and he added more wood to the fire, slept again, only to awaken, cold as before, to do it all over again. Finally, when Tilman woke, he noticed the mouth of the tunnel was no longer black, indistinguishable from the rest of the darkness. Now it was gray with the coming dawn. The fire was down to dead ashes, and he was stiff and aching from the cold. Quickly, he uncovered a few glowing coals, fed them splinters from the boxes, and soon had his fire built up again.

The storm had passed and in its wake a silence lay over the clean white mantle of snow as he crept to the entrance and studied the terrain outside the mine. There were no tracks in the snow that had drifted up around the tunnel opening. Making a quick scan of the area nearby, Tilman ducked down, moved behind his cover to a different place and scanned the middle distance. Nothing. Then, taking more time, he scanned the wide area, looking for unnatural movement and anything seeming out of place. Seeing nothing obviously amiss, he decided the sharpshooter was driven off by the storm and didn't remain overnight. Outside in the cold stillness, the only sound was the crunch of the powdery snow as Tilman made his way back up out of the cave. Everything was sharp and clear in the bright sunlight as he climbed up to where, the night before, he'd fired at the movement. Panting clouds of frosty breath, he found that the wind had blown the snow from a narrow bench. On closer examination, he saw four spent. 50 caliber brass cartridge cases, a broken laurel limb that he must have clipped with one of his shots, and on a nearby rock what could only be drops of dried blood. He picked up one of the cartridges, and pocketed it. Tilman knew then he'd hit someone with those hasty shots.

Going back to the tunnel and collecting his saddlebags, Tilman set out to walk back toward town. It was slow going crunching along in moccasins through the snow that had drifted several feet deep in places. As his feet grew numb he questioned what kind of Texan loses his horse and his boots and walks home? Well, in this case, a live one. He had made it through the night in one piece. Tilman smiled, in spite of the cold. Then he laughed out loud, glad to be alive.

Chapter Twenty-two

Tilman breathed cold clear mountain air, coughing as it burned his lungs, and then he stopped to look at the sky. The brown, rock-strewn mountain tops he'd grown accustomed to were now pristine white with newly fallen snow above the tree-line, and the snow blowing off the peaks reminded him of a wedding veil. Tilman's feet were numb—so how could they still ache with the cold if he'd lost feeling in them? He carried the Winchester bird-hunter style, with his hands jammed deep in his pockets, knowing that if anyone wanted to kill him, now would be the easiest time, for he could think only of the cold, eyes squinted almost shut against the blinding white of the snow. This was worse than winter in Amarillo. Those cowboys down there like to brag about working in the coldest weather. They used to say the only thing between Amarillo and the North Pole was a barbed wire fence! Tilman had news for them.

Coming up the trail below, a wondrous sight filled his snow-blinded eyes. Butter and Sheriff, leading Tilman's horse, appeared to be looking for him. Butter hallooed as soon as Tilman waved at them. Upon reaching Tilman, Butter pulled a blanket off his saddle, and Tilman was mighty grateful. The rescuers wanted to stop and build a fire, but Tilman said he'd rather get on down the hill. They rode back to Catherine's and Tilman was glad to step inside. Catherine had stoked up that big Franklin stove till it gave off heat like a slab of Texas hill country granite in August. Sitting as close as he could to the opening, clothes steaming, he began to warm up. Catherine couldn't hide her concern, and Tilman was sure he saw relief on her face when he stepped out of the mudroom and into her kitchen. Catherine served them all hot soup and coffee laced with sharp comments about people not having the sense God gave when it came to coming in out of the cold.

"I found out some things about Johnson," Sheriff said after Catherine had calmed down and gone to get seconds, "and about his servant. D'you know Johnson calls him his batman? That batman takes care of all Johnson's clothes an' ever' thing, even grooms Johnson's paint horse!"

"How did you find out all this?" Tilman asked as he inhaled the fresh cornbread that Catherine had placed next to the soup. He was starving.

"I was a good lawman, and make it my business to know things." Sheriff was enjoying being the center of attention in the small group. "That batman is right talkative, especially after a couple of drinks. Johnson was a second 'leftenant,' that's what the feller said, lef-tenant, in the British Army. His proper name is Neville Johnson, an' he is the second son of a Staffordshire gentleman." Sheriff rolled his eyes and made a kind of la-de-dah motion with his hands like he figured a proper English gentleman would. "But he got sent away from his reg'ment because he killed a man from London in a ruckus over gambling debts. The batman said Johnson welched on his IOUs. Now, in England, they got a tradition that the first son inherits everything, the second one goes to the Army, and the third boy becomes a preacher. That's the way they do it over there. O'course, his daddy wouldn't take him back in after that."

"Did he tell you that too?"

"Naw, I figured it out on my own," he said proudly. "Well, I'd read that's how the English do such family things. By the way, his batman told me he hisself was a corporal in the Army."

"Thanks, Sheriff."

What part did this Englishman have in this? From what Tilman knew, he'd sided with Ward against Dan, and James didn't like him. Tilman pulled out the .50 caliber casing he'd picked up earlier that morning at Shorty's firing position outside the mine. Digging out the other two he had, the one Morris gave him and the one he and Butter had found up by Five Elks, it was easy to see the firing pin marks and ejector marks were the same on all three. He quietly pointed out that fact to Butter, Sheriff, and Catherine, who studied the brass as carefully as he had. He knew then, as he suspected, Shorty was the man he sought.

"Shorty killed Dan," he said, "I'm sure of it, and now I am going to go get him."

He looked at Catherine. There was a surprised look on her face, but she quickly regained her composure.

"Tilman, is this really necessary? Can't you swear out a warrant and let the law take care of it now?"

"Catherine, you know how things work around here as well as I do. If it ever came to trial, he'd get no more than a fine and be back on the streets before I was." Tilman was aware of her concern. "If anything is to be done, justice to be served, as Dan's father the responsibility falls on my shoulders. Because the people here have allowed their police and courts to become corrupt, I must act."

"Tilman," she said and stepped close to him and put her hand on his arm. "What would your Sarah say to this?"

The warmth of her hand, the tenderness in the gesture, gave Tilman pause. If he went he could be killed. But the thought lasted only for a moment. "Leave her out of this. I owe it to Dan. It's the one last thing I can do for him."

"No. The thing you can do for him is to live a just and

honorable life. That's what he would want. That's what he would respect."

Tilman's mind was made up. He refused to argue the point.

"I'm going."

"If you must, let me at least offer you a warm coat," she said, going to a cedar chest and pulling out a wool blanket coat, "but maybe you'd rather freeze."

"I'm sorry, Catherine. I didn't mean to jump. I know you are worried for me. But I've got to go to town," Tilman said, while taking the coat. "Thank you for the added warmth. It will come in handy."

"It was my husband's." Her shoulders slumped with resignation. "You'll find there are gloves in the pockets."

When Tilman pulled out the gloves, a small book fell out with them. He looked and saw it was a pocket Bible that had belonged to Catherine's husband. Tilman stuck it back in his pocket as he didn't know what else to do with it, his mind already on the confrontation to come.

Unable to rest, he was determined that now was the time to have a showdown with Ward. Tilman told Sheriff and Butter what he had in mind and they said they'd go to town and back his play.

Catherine stood by Tilman's horse. Somewhere in the last few days and weeks their relationship had begun to change. She couldn't put her finger on when. All she knew was some place along the way, this man had walked into her life, and become an important element in her future.

Thinking how close she had come to getting involved with Bill Ward, even though she had always known that he was too smooth to be true, she shuddered.

"Catherine, a woman lets her good sense go when she has the problems of the world on her shoulders." Tilman's dark eyes seemed to see into her mind. She wondered how he knew what she was thinking.

"What do you mean, Tilman?" Catherine sputtered, blushing to the roots of her hair, sighing in frustration. "I must have been walking in my sleep. I never thought money and fine trappings were that important. How could I have let myself be so tempted?" She smiled at her own foolishness.

"You would have done the right thing, Catherine." Tilman reached out, unconsciously, brushing a loose curl out of her face. All at once it was quiet and time seemed to stand still. Gazing at each other, both were aware that after today things could never go back to where they had been between the two of them.

Catherine placed her hand on Tilman's hand, holding it gently against her face. Neither of them dared move. "Be safe, Tilman Wagner. Take care of yourself." She quickly turned and faced the distant snow-capped mountain range so she wouldn't see Tilman ride away and he didn't see the tears falling down her cheeks.

Chapter Twenty-three

Sheriff, unarmed, wanted to stop by the livery office to get his gun belt before looking for Shorty. Light flooded the interior of the building when the men opened the doors and walked towards the office. They found a saddle on the tack rail, and a closer examination revealed dried blood.

"This saddle goes with that paint pony in the first stall," Sheriff said.

"That looks a lot like the horse I saw up by Five Elks," Butter offered, "where that long shooter was practicing."

"Fellers," Sheriff said, "that animal belongs to the Englishman, Johnson."

"Are you sure?" Tilman quizzed Sheriff. This might change things a bit.

"O' course I am," Sheriff said, clearly offended that his memory was in question about a thing like horseflesh.

Tilman quickly reviewed the facts. Identical brass cartridge cases found in the rocks overlooking the station office where Dan was killed, at Five Elks, and where a man tried to kill him yesterday. The paint horse Butter saw at Five Elks was Johnson's horse. The shooter who left blood on the rocks yesterday, could that be his blood on Johnson's saddle? Tilman thought it was Shorty who tried to kill him yesterday.

This was not the horse Shorty rode when he followed Tilman into the mountains! Could Johnson be the man he sought? Were both men out there tracking him last night, and did Ward hire Johnson to shoot Dan, and then to try to kill him?

All three turned as a small man opened the office door and came to where they stood looking at the saddle. In his hands were a can of saddle soap, cloth rags, and a bucket of water.

"Beg pardon, gentlemen, but I've work to do here."

An Englishman!

"This here's Johnson's batman," Sheriff explained.

So that was who did it. Feeling cold inside, Tilman's actions were deliberate. This was no time to pussyfoot around, so he crowded close and put his face near to the batman's, nose-to-nose, and Tilman's voice fairly hissed with menace. "Answer quick and answer straight if you want to walk out of here in one piece. Does your boss have a .50 caliber Sharps rifle?"

The man gulped, and nodded assent.

"Was that you and him practicing at Five Elks?"

"Y-yes," he stuttered, "it was."

"Where was he yesterday?"

"I'm afraid I don't know." The poor frightened man's face was pale as death. "He left early in the day and returned late last night. He'd been hurt, so I cleaned his wound and bandaged his ear."

"Where is he now?" Tilman pushed his gun under the little man's chin so that his eyes bulged.

"He has rooms at the Silver King. I left him there."

"Keep him here, Sheriff, I don't want him warning Johnson."

The man who tried to kill Tilman yesterday on the mountain was *not* Shorty. It was *Johnson*. The truth had come out; finally, the end was in sight. Tilman's mind was in turmoil as he walked quickly through the muddy street to the Silver King, Butter trying unsuccessfully to keep up. Tilman was about to get the vengeance he wanted so badly. Stepping onto the boardwalk he slipped the hammer thong off his Colt then smashed the saloon's bat-wing doors open with such force one broke off the hinges and fell clattering into the room. The piano player gave a start, turned to look over his shoulder and his eyes met Tilman's. The man saw deadly intent in Tilman's hard eyes, for suddenly the music trailed off when the man stood, closed the cover over the keys, and like a whipped dog with his tail tucked between his legs, slunk from the room. The bartender slowly put down the glass he was polishing and his hands dropped behind the bar.

"You," Tilman said pointing at the barkeep, "throw that shotgun you keep back there out here. Hold it by the barrel, and do it slowly."

The bartender did as he was told, dropped his shotgun onto the floor in front of the bar and stepped away. Tilman found Blas, as expected, on the lookout, standing by the end of the bar where he could watch Shorty, who was drinking at the other end.

Looking around, Tilman saw Johnson, a fresh bandage wrapped around his head, bloodstained over his left ear. Johnson's batman had not lied. Tilman walked over to where Ward and Johnson were sitting at a table near the bar. Ward sat up straight in his chair, watched the tall man's approach, his eyes suddenly alert, evil, like a rattlesnake when it coils before striking. Ward was smoking a cheroot, and there was a half-full bottle of mescal in front of him with an empty shot glass by his hand. There was a steaming teapot in the middle of the table. Johnson was sipping from a delicate cup, and when he saw Tilman glaring at him his hand began shaking so badly tea splashed over the side and the cup rattled loudly as the Englishman placed it on the saucer.

Tilman looked down at Johnson's bandaged head; saw that the man's normally pale skin was gray, colorless, like that of a corpse. Tilman was sure Johnson was the one he'd wounded on the mountain after Shorty rode away.

"How did you get that wound?"

"Why are you questioning Mister Johnson?" Ward shoved his chair back as he stood, not wanting to be forced to have to look up at Tilman. "You've no right to accuse him of anything. Get out of my place. I told you already that you aren't wanted in this town. Not by Catherine, me, or anybody. Your boy is dead and gone and nothing should be keeping you here. So why don't you smarten up and get out now." He paused, sat back down, and then added, "While you can."

"I'm not accusing him of anything yet," Tilman said watching Johnson's eyes, "I just want to know what happened to him." Without looking at Ward, Tilman said, "You stay out of this. Now, Johnson, I'll ask you one more time—how did you get that wound?"

"The Granite Gang drygulched him yesterday morning," Ward said quickly, "and he's been here in the Silver King recovering ever since." Johnson remained seated. Refusing to look Tilman in the eye, he fiddled nervously with his teaspoon.

"I told you to keep your mouth shut," said Tilman, whose voice was barely above a whisper as he palmed his waist pistol with his left hand and pressed the muzzle against the middle of Ward's forehead. In the sudden quiet, the sound of the hammer cocking back practically thundered through the room.

"Ward, this thing has a hair trigger, so if you move, you're dead." Still looking at Johnson, Tilman asked, "Do you own a .50 caliber Sharps?"

Sweat broke out on Johnson's forehead.

"Aren't you the one who set up a practice range out by Five Elks? My boy Dan found out about Ward's plan to rob the treasure wagon and wouldn't go along with it, so Ward here hired you to kill my son, didn't he? Answer me!" Tilman shouted.

"I say, you've no right . . ." he protested feebly. "Shorty," he cried desperately, "go get help." Wild-eyed, Johnson turned to Ward. Shorty, who couldn't bring himself to look at Johnson, tried to pour another drink, but his hand shook so badly he sloshed more whiskey onto the bar than went into his glass. Why hadn't Johnson learned that men like Shorty only look out for themselves? There was a saying that no honor existed among thieves. Apparently Johnson hadn't heard that over in England. Too bad.

The saloon was as silent as a tomb, all eyes riveted on the scene now unfolding, watching with fascinated certainty that someone was about to die before them in an explosion of noise, gun smoke, and blood. Yet for all their fear they were unable to tear their eyes away.

"It was you tried to kill me yesterday up above Harvard City, wasn't it?" Tilman demanded. "You killed my son for Ward, didn't you?"

"Bill, help me!" Johnson pleaded on the verge of panic.

"Shut up, you fool!" Ward ordered.

Then, making a high keening sound from his throat, a sound of abject, animal fear, Johnson tried to stand while he made a desperate but awkward grab for a derringer inside his coat.

A bullet slammed into Johnson's chest through the top button of his vest, the sound of the shot coming from the front door of the saloon. Johnson crumpled loosely to the floor like a puppet whose strings had been cut, the small pistol clattering noisily, uselessly, across the wooden floor.

Distracted by the closeness of the bullet, Tilman involuntarily leaned back away from Johnson as he fell. Ward quickly pushed Tilman's pistol aside. Tilman tried to recover but for some reason everything seemed to be happening so slowly, yet he was able to see it all in amazing clarity! Tilman simply couldn't react fast enough. Ward took a step back, drew a nickel-plated pistol and at point-blank range shot Tilman in the chest.

The impact of the slug slammed Tilman backward onto a table, crashing it down to the floor. He lay still, stunned by the bullet's shock as a burning pain grew fiercely in the right side of his chest. As the shock wore off, pain flooded Tilman's mind. He groaned, ears ringing from the explosion of the shot. Tilman looked down to where the bullet entered, saw a smoking hole in his coat where a residue of gunpowder had stuck, burning red, the embers sending up curls of stinking smoke. Tilman looked expectantly, waiting for Sarah to appear. That was what he had always heard happened when one died, a loved one waited to help the dying across into the hereafter.

"Sheriff, drop that gun and come on in with your hands in the air," Ward said.

His voice seemed to Tilman to come from far away.

So it was Sheriff who had shot Johnson! Dimly, Tilman was aware that most of the customers had scurried shamelessly from the saloon, as had the serving girls, who screamed every step of the way. Blas kept his hands on the bar, but his eyes glittered like a stalking cat's as he studied the pistol Ward held.

"Call a doctor, somebody, please," Johnson's voice wheezed weakly from the floor near Tilman. "I'm shot through the lungs."

"You had the chance to end this yesterday but you failed," Ward said, as he kicked a whimpering Johnson in the side. "I was a fool to hire a Limey to do man's work. I should have let Shorty do it."

Tilman could hardly move, the pain burned like fire and he thought he could feel the grating of broken bones inside his chest with each ragged breath. Tilman watched with a feeling of detached helplessness as Ward aimed a pistol, ready to finish him off. So, this was it, the hour of his death had come.

"Amigo!" rang from the bar, surprising Ward, who turned his head to look while his gun was still held at Tilman's head. Blas stepped near, his gun drawn and pointed at Ward.

"You are Johnny Russell, from Silver City, and, *senor,* I

have you now. A-ah," he cautioned, "don't you move that *pistola, amigo*." Tilman watched in amazement as Blas playfully wagged his gun barrel at Ward, like a schoolteacher's finger when she corrects a misbehaving child. "I am a very careful *hombre*," Blas smiled coldly, "so you don't want to make me nervous. For over a year I have been following you, a *year* my friend, and now I am going to collect my reward. Hey," Blas taunted, "do you know your own mother put the reward on your head?" He smiled again, but not with his eyes. "No? Well, dead or alive she said, and it don't matter which to me. So, *Juanito*, which will it be? I don't want to kill you, I promise, so why don't you make it easy on yourself and put down that gun?"

"Help me," Johnson once again moaned, his cries becoming faint.

"Hey, *amigo*, who is this boy?" Blas pointed at Johnson with his chin, "He is your hired gun, maybe?"

"He's nobody," Ward snapped back. "He claimed he was a killer and he could shoot, but he lied. It turns out his conscience bothered him and he wanted out," he sneered. "You, Mex, how much is the reward? I'll double it! Triple it! I'm gonna be rich, richer than you ever dreamed! I own this town. You can have half of it if you'll side with me! Just you walk out that door and let me finish up here and we'll talk." Ward wanted to keep Blas talking while he tried desperately to think of something, anything he could do that might change the situation so he could get the drop on Blas. He was too close to the biggest job he'd ever pulled, respectability in his own town; he'd have it *all!* He couldn't fail now, could he? What could he do?

"I think you are a liar, *amigo*." Blas smiled agreeably.

There on the floor, Johnson, the would-be gunman for hire, looked at Tilman and died.

Ward uttered a small cry of desperation and tried to swing his gun around, but Blas, cold-eyed, looking ever more like the devil with his lips curled in the wicked half-smile Tilman had seen at Salida, shot Bill down. At such a shot range, less than five feet, only one shot would be needed. Blas never blinked as he fired until his gun was empty, the hammer falling finally on a spent shell. Ward fell heavily between Johnson and Tilman and lay unmoving as his last breath escaped his lips, his half-closed eyes looking upward at nothing. The acrid smell of gun smoke filled the room.

Blas's shots had been fired so close to Tilman they made his ears ring even more.

"Hey, *Juanito,* I lied, too, eh?" Blas said, quietly, holstering the empty gun and producing another from the waistband of his trousers at the small of his back. "You can't trust nobody anymore."

Tilman felt vibrations through the floor, or maybe he heard footsteps when Shorty jumped up and made a drunken, staggering run for the door only to be intercepted there by Butter.

Tilman sat up, still a little dazed. Why wasn't he dead? He put his hand into the jacket under the powder-burned bullet hole, a finger searching to explore the wound. Tilman had seen enough gunshot wounds in the war and on the frontier to know what was fatal and what was not. He opened his shirt. There was no wound! Instead he found a small, angry indentation on his chest, a dark purplish bruise beginning around it. The sharp, knifing pain of a broken rib inside told Tilman he had not completely escaped harm. What happened to the bullet? From the breast pocket of the jacket he pulled out the pocket Bible. He smiled in amazed relief, for the pistol ball was imbedded in the book.

When he looked up he saw Catherine, fear in her eyes, step into the room. She hesitated, for surely she had never been in a saloon before, but then with courage born of desperation, she ran to Tilman's side, dropping to her knees.

"How bad is it?"

"What are you doing here? This is no place for a lady," Tilman sputtered when she began to search for the wound.

"Tilman!" she scolded.

Where had he heard that before? "Look," he said as he held up the Bible with the bullet stuck in it.

Her face lit up with a relieved smile as she leaned back. Completely unaware that she was on the floor in the town's newest saloon with two dead bodies lying alongside, she said, "I thought you Wagners were hard-headed, but now I have proof! Are you sure it didn't hit your head first and bounce off that?"

"I've had more compassion from an old camp cook!" he gasped. It hurt more than he wanted to let on.

"Oh," a tear welled up in her eyes, "you know what I mean."

The batman came into the room and knelt by Johnson.

"'E's not really a hired gunman," he explained, sadly. "'E got carried away with the Wild West stories, an' passed 'imself off as a killer. 'Is family couldn't control 'im in England an' they sent me to keep an eye on 'im." He covered Johnson's face with a white silk handkerchief. "I'm afraid I let them down."

Tilman saw that Johnson, sprawled dead on the saloon floor, no longer wore his fancy silver spurs.

Chapter Twenty-four

Tilman was in no shape for traveling. Catherine asked Butter and Sheriff to bring Tilman to his room in her home to recover from a bruised and sore chest and a broken rib. The trip to Catherine's home, in the back of a wagon with Needles following behind, was not one he wanted to repeat. Every frozen rut and every rock in the road jarred his ribs.

There had been a coroner's inquest with an honest ruling from a new coroner, which meant the town was on its way to establishing true law and order, a place where the expectation and the guarantee of justice improved the quality of life. Maybe now citizens could turn to the law with confidence rather than have to take matters into their own hands as Tilman had done. The doctor had ridden out to the house, pronounced Tilman generally sound, but admonished him to not move for at least a week or so as the broken rib had irritated one of his older wounds. Tilman still carried around pieces of an old bullet from the war under that side of his rib cage, and while it was no problem most of the time the bullet's impact had set it to hurting as well. Resting in the solitude of his room Tilman took a long, hard look at his life and thought about what had happened.

According to Sheriff, Blas, sporting a new set of silver spurs with jinglebobs, had the Mahonville chief constable certify that Ward, or Russell going by his real name, was wanted for murder in New Mexico and was "killed attempting to evade capture." That cleared the way for the Silver City sheriff to pay Blas his bounty. It also got rid of Blas. No one had any desire to have him remain, as there was an empty evilness that surrounded him that made people look over their shoulders. Within a week Shorty was returned to Durango in irons to stand trial for his part in the ore theft and murder of a mine guard. The last thing anybody heard, a mob in Durango was threatening to drag Shorty out of the jailhouse and string him up.

As Tilman saw it, every man, good or bad, had the power to choose his path, and there were always going to be battles in life because some so-and-so chose to do wrong. On the other hand, there would always be peace for those who chose to walk a straight path. But even when a man had one, be it battle or blessing, the other was not far off. He thought long and hard about settling down, but to do that he'd have to let go of the only life he knew and start all over. For a man his age that wouldn't be easy.

He'd finally learned the truth and exacted his revenge on the men responsible for Dan's death. But revenge was hollow. It wouldn't bring back Dan, just as it hadn't brought back Sarah.

What about his feelings for Catherine? And what about the boy? Honestly, the feelings were there, but were Catherine and James more a replacement for Sarah and Dan than love? He wasn't sure, and knew he couldn't think about trying to settle down with Catherine until he was absolutely certain it was right. His doubts were interrupted when a smiling Pastor Fry, two steaming mugs of strong coffee in hand, stepped into the room to visit.

Tilman sipped the dark brew and his eyes widened. "Why, Pastor, there's more than just coffee in here!"

"A body needs a taste of something to fight off a chill these cold days," he laughed.

"Paul, I'm working really hard trying to decipher what all of this is about." Tilman sipped his coffee for a moment. "My boy is avenged, but he is still not here with me. He's gone. Two more men dead and a third will soon join them. The law on Earth—an eye for an eye—is complete, but why doesn't that fill the big void I have in my heart for my boy? I blamed everybody but myself for the guilt that I carried around for Sarah and Dan and not being where I should have been."

"You're going to have to let go of the past, Tilman. If you don't, you will worry about what might have been for the rest of your life. Doubts and remorse will eat you all hollow inside," the Pastor spoke quietly. "When you're ready, I can help you choose your path and move on."

Catherine had insisted that Tilman's chair and footstool be set up close by a window so he could feel the sunlight and see the sky. The warmth he now experienced came not from sunlight but from the depths of his weary soul. Was there a chance to come to terms with the burden of guilt he'd imposed upon himself and then carried like a banner in his own private war for too many years? Tilman faced the Pastor. "Do you think there's a chance for a man who has lived like I have?"

"There is." He paused, as if unsure as to what to say and then started to smile. "In fact," he began to chuckle, "let me share with you the main reason why I came." He was still laughing when he began to tell his tale.

"I opened my Bible this morning and I immediately thought of you because I turned to the passage that says 'I have plans for you.'"

Before Tilman could respond Catherine came in the room. Just back from the town, her cheeks reddened by a cool wind, she was a breath of fresh air. James ran in ahead of her, and stood beside Tilman.

"Mister Tilman, Mister Tilman, you'll never guess."

"Whoa! Hold on boy. One word at a time."

"One of those boys from town tried to beat me up again and I held my arms up the way you showed me." He made a show of getting his hands up in front of his face, elbows tucked in, crouched to protect his belly, just as Tilman had shown him. "Well, it hurt his hands like you said, but it hurt *my* arms too, but I didn't let on." He grinned. "When he saw I wasn't afraid of him, he got scared! I took one step to get closer to him and he ran away crying for his ma!"

"You've created a monster, Tilman." Catherine rolled her eyes, saying, "No boy in town is safe now."

"No *bully* is safe, you mean." Turning to James, Tilman smiled and said, "Son, you've learned a good lesson today. You'll find there are some people who play the tough and push others around because that's the only way they know to behave. Now that boy knows you won't push, maybe you can be friends."

"Go out to the spring house and get me that crock of cream, then wash up," Catherine said shooing James out of the room, "and I'll make you some gingerbread.

"Tilman, I saw Miss Alma at the general store, and she asked me to tell you that she hoped you wouldn't be too upset, but Jackie, the store clerk is courting her now. Alma's sorry, but you're too old for her and it wouldn't be seemly if you persisted." She said all that with a straight face. "She's the happiest woman in the world!" Catherine broke out laughing, the strain of the last few days slowly receding in her memory. "You're quite the heartbreaker, Mister Wagner."

Starting to protest, Tilman realized she was joking, even if it was at his expense, so he joined in the laughter. For the first time in years, he wasn't shackled to hate anymore.

"Oh, I almost forgot. I also saw Sheriff was going to ride out here with this, but I saved him a trip." Catherine handed Tilman a telegram, and then stood behind his chair, her hands warm and gentle on Tilman's shoulders. The way a wife would stand, Tilman thought.

Opening the telegram, Tilman found it was an urgent message from John Law, one of his fellow Confederates from North Carolina, now serving in the Yankee Army at Fort Davis, Texas. John's daughter and the post's schoolmistress had been captured by a mixed band of Mexican bandits and Indian raiders and were being held for ransom. The Army couldn't cross the Mexican border, but a man like Tilman would be under no such constraints.

Pastor Fry took the telegram to read. He chuckled as he handed the telegram back to Tilman. "Remember what I just said about plans?" Tilman smiled and stood up. Catherine sputtered something about only a crazy man would travel when he's not well, and Tilman laughed again, joined by Pastor Fry.

"You can get a work train out of South Arkansas tomorrow morning to connect to the main line at Pueblo," Pastor Fry said.

"Butter's on the treasure run to Como. When he returns, tell him what happened and that I had to go, but I'm much obliged for all his help," Tilman said. "I couldn't have done this without his help and friendship."

Catherine looked at Tilman, started to speak but changed her mind. Shrugging her shoulders, she headed for the kitchen but stopped in the doorway, her eyes locked on Tilman's. "Let us know how you are and what happens." Her voice was thin, strained. "I'm sure James will want to know."

Tilman blocked the doorway. "What about you, Catherine?"

"Sit down Tilman. You're not well yet!" she exclaimed as she tried to hide shaking hands beneath her apron. "Yes, I want to know too." Blushing, she turned and made off to the privacy of the kitchen.

A new part of Tilman's journey was revealed, and a new adventure beckoned.